Ransom & Ruin

Jesimae Book I

S.E. Zell

Copyright © 2023 by S.E. Zell

All rights reserved.

No portion of this book may be reproduced in any form without written permission from the publisher or author, except as permitted by U.S. copyright law.

Table of Contents

Author's Note	VI
Names	VII
Prologue	1
1. Chapter 1	4
2. Chapter 2	12
3. Chapter 3	19
4. Chapter 4	23
5. Chapter 5	27
6. Chapter 6	31
7. Chapter 7	34
8. Chapter 8	46
9. Chapter 9	51
10. Chapter 10	55
11. Chapter 11	61
12. Chapter 12	63
13. Chapter 13	69
14. Chapter 14	71

15. Chapter 15 — 74
16. Chapter 16 — 78
17. Chapter 17 — 80
18. Chapter 18 — 86
19. Chapter 19 — 89
20. Chapter 20 — 92
21. Chapter 21 — 95
22. Chapter 22 — 102
23. Chapter 23 — 104
24. Chapter 24 — 109
25. Chapter 25 — 113
26. Chapter 26 — 118
27. Chapter 27 — 121
28. Chapter 28 — 126
29. Chapter 29 — 128
30. Chapter 30 — 132
31. Chapter 31 — 141
32. Chapter 32 — 144
33. Chapter 33 — 149
34. Chapter 34 — 153
35. Chapter 35 — 157
36. Chapter 36 — 159
37. Chapter 37 — 163

38.	Chapter 38	169
39.	Chapter 39	175
40.	Chapter 40	181
41.	Chapter 41	187
42.	Chapter 42	191
43.	Chapter 43	195
44.	Chapter 44	199
45.	Chapter 45	204
46.	Chapter 46	213
47.	Chapter 47	218
48.	Chapter 48	222
	Epilogue	225
	Jesimae Book II	228
	Let's Connect!	231
	Thank you!	232

Author's Note

This is a fully edited, revised, and expanded edition of my 2016 novel, *Jesimae*. After many years off from writing, I knew I had to revisit this world of my own making and make it even better, if I could. If you are here for the first time, welcome and thank you so much for being a part of this epic journey—these siblings need all the allies they can get. If you are here for the second time…shh no spoilers! But thank you for returning. Thank you all for your support, enjoy the adventure, and please come back for book 2 in December 2023!

Names

Aedrian—AY-dree-an

Aedrik—AY-drik

Ashdan—ASH-den

Baela—BAY-luh

Besian—BEE-zee-en

Calloway—CAL-o-way or just Cal

Daeva—DAY-vuh

Deorick—dee-OR-ick

Emyr—EM-er

Kilian—KILL-ee-en

Silvija—sil-VEE-uh

Prologue
The Daeva

"I should have killed you the minute you walked in here," drawled King Besian of Jesimae.

The Daeva sauntered over to the chair on the other side of the king's desk and sank into the plush cushions before responding, "You've had plenty of chances to kill me over the years, Besian. And yet, here I am. I thought for sure when you banished me after your wife's death, that would be the last I'd hear from you. Pray tell, what drove you to call on me after nearly three decades?"

They sat back in the seat, waiting for his answer. Besian "The Conqueror" was a hard and unforgiving man. It had pleasantly surprised the Daeva to receive a summons from the King of this embittered and war-torn land.

In their youth, the two had been close. The Daeva had been instrumental in Besian's strategic marriage and his conquering of the northern territories. They often mourned the loss of those early, bloodthirsty days.

"Well?"

"That upstart in the Black City, Angerona. What's his name...Aedrik. He's still calling himself King of Thieves?"

The Daeva felt a sneer of derision cross their face at the mention of their enemy. "Of the Western half anyway."

"Indeed," he said, acknowledging that the Daeva ruled the eastern half of Jesimae's criminal underworld. "Indeed. I've had enough of his posturing.

He's an arrogant, irreverent, and spoiled child—" He cut off as if trying to rein in his more virulent emotions.

"I won't disagree with you, Majesty. Go on." The formality in their voice and the subtle flash of red that lit up the crimson glyphs on their arms told the king he might be better off getting to the point. The Daeva already knew all of these things about Aedrik and had no interest in sitting around complaining about him.

Besian always had a tendency to stick his nose where it wasn't wanted. His subjects faced some serious neglect as the king spewed vitriol about a twenty-something common thief.

"I want the boy dead."

"That's it?"

"Well, not entirely."

"Of course not."

"I want him discredited and his 'empire' torn apart. I can't have a commoner—a half-breed no less—thinking he is on equal footing with me. It will give the people ideas and we've only just stifled the northern rebellion."

The Daeva studied the king for a moment, choosing to ignore the racial slur against the people of which they were a full-blooded member, before asking, "When do you want to start?"

"Soon," he replied, eyes simmering with malice and a touch of madness. "Before we start the Royal Progress. By the time we reach Angerona, I want him ground to dust."

The Daeva smiled. There weren't many people who felt free to express themselves as such in front of them, but Besian had always been dear to them. Besides, why deny the man when their desires were one and the same?

"Very well. I expect the proper payment and reinstatement in your court after the deed is complete."

"Done."

Chapter 1
Aedrik

Four months later.

Aedrik was sprawled sideways across the arms of his ebony throne. It was a beautifully carved stone seat that he liked to think was as grand as the one that tyrant who called himself King sat on down in the Capital. The stark room was currently empty except for him. His sister had dubbed it the Vault when it became his base of operations. Iron brackets were bolted to the wall and held torches burning with a steady blue flame. The only furniture in the room was a round obsidian table and four chairs including the one he currently draped himself across.

His long jet-black hair nearly brushed the cold floor and his eyes closed in utter exhaustion as he daydreamed. He would be the last to admit it, but after expending the amount of power he had in the last few months, fine lines had started to appear around his eyes and mouth. He was none too happy with the physical toll, but couldn't discount the fruits of his labor.

After months of hard work, the final piece of his plan had fallen into place. All that was left was to set it in motion.

He opened an ice blue eye at the sound of the lift grinding to a halt outside the door. A simple flex of the powers that were his birthright would have told him who was about to enter the room, but he was unable to summon the energy. The markings on his arms merely flickered blue before fading back to black. He was by no means helpless, being just as deadly with his bare hands as he was with a spell, but only four people alive could even access this room, including him. If *they* meant him harm, he was well and truly fucked.

"I guess the Key is complete, then?" His twin's voice interrupted the peaceful musings on his own excellence and he groaned as he sat up. "You look like shit," Aedrian grinned as he took the seat to Aedrik's right.

"Yes. It took more effort than I initially thought, but it should be able to get you in anywhere. I have to say, it's probably my finest work to date." He smirked and watched Aedrian's cobalt eyes roll. Apart from the slight difference in their eye color and the scars they'd accumulated over the years, Aedrik and Aedrian were identical in every way. Tall, with broad shoulders and jet-black hair, the young men commanded attention wherever they went. Their father used to say they were too pretty to make it very far in the criminal underworld. Of course, that was right before Aedrik had battled him to the death for the title of Rogue.

Aedrik won, gaining him the title and a fresh scar over his right eye, while their father gained a new home—six feet under the cracked and barren ground outside this forsaken city.

Aedrian had taken over as Aedrik's second in command, sometimes causing a bit of confusion when people were addressing them. They had considered masquerading as the same person so that Aedrik would seem all powerful, but they were already too well known in Angerona. That and Aedrian lacked the angry red scar that had still been healing on Aedrik's face at the time.

People in the brothers' domain worshipped them with equal parts love and fear, never really knowing which twin was more dangerous as Aedrian could be just as vicious as Aedrik when pushed.

"The others are on their way. I just heard from Ash. Apparently, she's finishing up a... personal matter," Aedrian said, shaking his head. Aedrik let out an incredulous snort. If Aedrian was Aedrik's right hand, their little sister, Ashdan, was the sinister left. Ashdan was the deadliest person he knew. She took care of any threats to their rule of Western Jesimae's underworld without leaving a single trace of evidence.

Ashdan had a fierce sense of justice and would give people one chance only to rehabilitate their ways. If they failed, they were found dead soon after with a bright red kiss on their cheek. Breaking the law was one thing, but harming Aedrik's loyal followers was something none of the siblings could stand for.

Just then, the grinding sound came again and the brothers' most trusted Lieutenant, Deorick, squeezed his gigantic body through the doorway. At a head taller than the doorframe, he was forced to stoop to avoid hitting his head. He was a full-blooded member of the mountainous Elymas people and the black markings that were only on the siblings' arms and shoulders covered his entire body, including his bald head and stern face. At the moment, some of those markings were obscured by rust-colored splatters of blood. Aedrik merely raised an eyebrow at his friend's appearance.

"Kilian's people were stirring things up again in the South District. I handled it."

Aedrik exchanged glances with his brother. Kilian was getting to be a problem. His attempts to incite violence around the city in lieu of actually challenging the brothers for their rule had been comical at first, but they would soon have to put him down permanently. Aedrik was sure Ashdan would volunteer for the task; Kilian's "riots" had caused several deaths of innocent bystanders. She would be itching by now to stick a knife in the bastard.

Speak of the devil…a rail-thin blonde in a tight dress complete with innocent-looking braids and wide blue eyes waltzed into the Chamber and plopped down in Ashdan's seat. She looked like something out of one of the lurid stories the old men sitting in the corners of pubs liked to tell.

"Ash, drop the glamour. You're among family and friends here."

The blonde pouted in a way that probably had most men bending over backwards to please her, but only made him cringe.

"I mean it."

She bared her teeth at the command in his voice, but morphed back into his mahogany-haired, green-eyed sister. The glyphs he could just see at the edges of her sleeves faded to black as the three men watched her wipe a spot of blood from her cheek.

"Apparently, that's become part of the team uniform," Aedrik said, gesturing to her now red-smeared face. Despite the blood, Ashdan was still completely put together—almost annoyingly so. She was exceptionally gifted with deception magic. It had been her favorite game to try and fool her brothers when they were younger, though their mental connection made it kind of difficult to get anything past them. When she got older, it had become part of the avenging angel persona she created, the Red Lady. No one knew what the Lady looked like, so you had better be on your best behavior because you would never see her coming. Ashdan had been delighted when she learned that the Red Lady was also used as a cautionary tale for children. In her mind, she was "preventing the disloyalty of the next generation."

"Now that we're all here, let's begin." Aedrik reached under his shirt and pulled out the Skeleton Key he'd created. He placed the small octagon on the table in front of him for everyone to see. From each point of the octagon, the metal curved upward to meet in a spiral at the center. There were glyphs carved in between each section, imbuing the object with Aedrik's magic. When he glanced at Aedrian's face, he immediately knew what his twin was thinking.

"Don't even say it."

"It's just that-"

"No."

"-You've been talking about it all this time-"

"Stop it."

Ashdan snickered, knowing what was coming.

"It's a bit...smaller than I expected." His smirk said it all. Aedrik narrowed his eyes, giving his brother a glare that stopped most people cold. Unfortunately, his twin was all but immune to the Rogue's hard edges.

Ever the practical one, Deorick spoke up before things could get more juvenile, "Does it work?" Aedrik stroked the intricate symbols carved in the dark wood and shot the other man a baleful glance. Yes, it worked perfectly.

"Have I ever created something that doesn't?" The markings mimicked some of the ones on their bodies and he could feel those corresponding glyphs shiver across his skin in recognition.

"So what now?" This from Ashdan who was looking decidedly bored. "You've had this super secret-project for months. Do *we* actually get to do something now?"

Aedrik waved a tired hand over the glassy surface of the table, but nothing happened. He was tapped out. He gestured to his sister. With an arched brow and look of mild concern, Ashdan repeated his gesture and floor plans of the Angeronian Governor's Palace appeared in the gloom. With that, Aedrik began to outline the plan:

"The King's annual progress will be stopping in Angerona for the first time in forever in just a few days. Most of the time, the King avoids our unruly corner of his empire. Probably to try to prove to me that we're not significant enough to warrant his meddling.

This trip works in our favor because the Capital darling, Crown Prince Emyr, is traveling with the retinue. Using the key, Aedrian and Ashdan will be able to enter the Governor's Palace undetected. The Royal guests sleep in the Keep on the far corner of the Palace grounds, closest to the service gate and the cliffs that overlook the harbor.

Thanks to a couple of inside men, you two can capture the Crown Prince and transport him to the family fortress in the Licean Mountains. Mom is expecting you. There, we'll hold him for ransom until I'm able to leverage the identity of the Eastern Rogue out of King Besian."

The Eastern Rogue. Or the Daeva, as most called them, was a complete unknown. Only the King of Jesimae had ever met the Daeva in person and could tell Aedrik who had been encroaching on his territory and ambushing his people for the last four months. That was why a few months ago Aedrik had started working on a plan to uncover the Daeva's identity and confront this hidden nemesis.

That was the plan, but all four of them knew that anything could go wrong and were more than prepared to fight and magic their way out of a tight situation. In fact, Aedrik figured these three would probably relish a good bloody battle. Possible treachery was also the reason that only six people in the world knew of the plan—four of which were in the room presently. One of the others might as well be blood and would never let anything slip, while the other had been spelled to keep the secret and offered a handsome reward in return for his services.

"So step one: the kidnapping is where the key comes in. It can only be used once in a short period of twelve hours because it will need to recharge. You won't be able to get into the wing where the royal family is staying through the palace. Too many opportunities to be seen. You will enter through the Servants' Gate."

Aedrik pointed to a tiny square on the edge of the map.

"The wall to the Keep is here near the stables and from there you can temporarily create the door that will give you access to the bottom floor.

Ashdan, I'm sure you'll find a way past the guards outside the Prince's door."

"I've already made up a goody basket," she responded with a thin smile. Aedrik cringed slightly at her gleeful response. Ashdan loved to experiment with poisons, but she tended to go overboard in her measurements and had nearly killed all of them on several occasions. She was more precise than a needle with a blade, but her skill with herbs and concoctions might as well be like that of a cudgel. He did not want to be the recipient of anything she put in that basket, but damn was he glad she was on their side.

"Try not to kill anyone this time. I've managed all this time as Rogue to not develop a reputation for wanton murder. I don't wish to start now. We've got an old friend on the inside too, so try not to break him before you recognize him." His gaze bored into Ashdan.

Aedrian cut in. "Don't worry, I gave her the ingredients and measured everything out. No one's dying on my watch."

Aedrik felt a wave of instant relief. Ashdan may not have a knack for anything to do with plants and animals, but Aedrian could sing to a seedling and have it feeding you ripe apples by nightfall.

"Also, remember, you all have to be out of there in ten minutes. That's how long the key will be able to keep the door open if you set it to its highest setting. It's not meant to be permanent, so no horsing around."

Ashdan sighed and gave him an innocent look that said, "Have we *ever* let you down?" Aedrik didn't dignify that with an answer. Anything could go wrong when you were committing treason.

"Then it's set. Tomorrow night, we strike." Deorick cracked his large knuckles in anticipation. After they talked through the rest of the plan, Aedrian swept the key from under Aedrik's fingers and into his tunic while Ashdan rose from her chair. Aedrik's hand waved in dismissal and the other three filed out, Aedrian tugging on their sister's long hair to pull her into a conversation and Deorick climbing silently on to the lift behind them. The grinding of the stone platform signaled their departure and Aedrik was left alone, brimming with equal parts worry and anticipation.

He sprawled sideways once again and let his hand drift over the cold dust-strewn floor. He shut his eyes and started humming an old song he remembered from his youth about blood being spilt so that justice can be done. Tomorrow *his* quest for justice would begin. Those insects playing dress up in cloaks of power would know before the week was out who was really in charge.

Chapter 2

Emyr

Crown Prince Emyr lay in bed listening to the sounds of the camp stirring in the early morning light outside his tent. He had barely slept, haunted by the nagging feeling that this last stop on the Royal Progress was his father's worst idea yet. Angerona, the City of Thieves, was easily the most dangerous place in Jesimae, if not the Five Kingdoms. Every horror story from his youth started with, "A long time ago, in the Black City of Angerona..." The dizzying patterns sewn into the fabric of his tent and the comfortable cocoon of blankets he'd wrapped himself in allowed his mind to wander aimlessly through his memories, recalling every story he'd heard about Angerona and its deadly inhabitants.

Emyr was glad when Barrett and Calloway entered his tent and interrupted his thoughts. His two personal guards were a study in contrasts. Calloway was lean with white blonde hair and fair skin while Barrett's head was shaved and his skin was a deep cocoa only a few shades darker than Emyr's own. Living on the southern coast of Jesimae, in the Capital, had given all three of them a ruddy glow that could only come from countless hours spent outdoors and on the water. Quiet Calloway often went unnoticed next to Barrett's commanding presence, but Emyr often suspected that Calloway was the more dangerous of the two. It was the barrel-chested Southerner's booming voice, however, that pulled him out of his half-doze state every morning. Today was no exception.

"Majesty, it's time for us to pack up the camp and move on to the next stop in the Progress. It will take half a day to reach Angerona and your father wishes to be inside the Governor's Palace well before nightfall."

"For once, I agree with him. I wouldn't want to be caught on those streets after dark," Emyr grumbled as he picked up his sword belt. It was a comfort to have the thing around his waist when embarking on what he considered to be a completely idiotic endeavor. That and his bow and arrows made him feel confident he could face whatever came their way, but that feeling of dread still wouldn't go away, making him worry that something truly terrible was coming.

Barrett's voice cut in again.

"What'd you say Blondie? Quit mumbling over there."

Calloway scowled at Barrett.

"I said the streets of Angerona aren't that bad if you know how to navigate them."

"And I assume you're speaking from experience. Right, Cal?" Emyr was half-joking but genuinely curious. He knew almost nothing personal about the quieter of his two guards except that he didn't like being called Cal by his superiors. He wanted to see if he could eke anything else out of the man because that also happened to be one of the longest sentences Calloway had ever uttered in his presence.

The wiry shoulders shrugged, "It's not all bad." He seemed to have used up his ration of words for the day because he looked uncomfortable and quickly turned away to start packing some of Emyr's things.

Emyr felt his left eyebrow struggling to reach his hairline. He knew Calloway was from somewhere northwest of the Capital, Tsifira, but could it be that Calloway had honed the craft that had saved Emyr's own life on several occasions on the rough streets of the Thieves' City? Emyr supposed it made a weird sort of sense. The man was silent as air and fought ruthlessly, without honor. It was entirely possible that Calloway had learned those things out of necessity on the streets of the Black City.

That thought brought back the knot in his gut as he set about helping to pack up his things and saddling his horse. His father may think that doing actual work was beneath him, but Emyr had always believed a Prince should gain all the practical skills he could so he would never be helpless. The Palace servants had been surprised over the years when the Crown Prince of Jesimae would approach them asking to be taught the basics of their craft, but they had soon grown into their roles as instructors and wouldn't let him give up until he could do it right.

It was continually evident to Emyr that his father only went on these annual Royal Progresses in order to flaunt his power and wealth, not to greet the people and hear their problems. It was especially apparent in territories that they had conquered within Besian's reign and where their hold was more tenuous.

Emyr mounted his horse, Baela, with his guards following behind him and rode to meet the King at the head of the riotously colored column. The members of the Royal Court bowed low where they stood or rode as he passed them by. He almost had to laugh at how uncomfortable they all were. It served them right, wearing silks and finery as they travelled through a dusty and barren desert. Many had holes in the bottoms of their delicate shoes and had been complaining before they noticed his approach of blisters and riding sores. Emyr shook his head and adjusted his simple, yet well-made, traveling clothes before continuing on to where his father waited.

"Emyr! My boy! Good of you to join us!" King Besian had a knack for making people feel like they had done something wrong even when they hadn't. Emyr sometimes joked that he was King of the Back-handed Compliment. The look in his eyes told Emyr that he had hoped his son would join them sooner. His father motioned toward Baron Nigel of Licea mounted on a fine grey mare next to him. The small mousy man had been using the Royal Progress as an opportunity to spout undue praise into the King's ear.

As the ruler of one of the smaller and more desolate territories in Jesimae, Nigel had seen his chance to get into the King's good graces and hadn't left Besian's side in the months since. Emyr knew his father couldn't stand the man and occasionally felt a little sympathetic towards Besian's plight. The man kept on incessantly, but the King valued the relationships he had with his nobles; even the ones with Lordlets of territories hardly worth mentioning. One never knew when the mountainous region and bleak Eastern coast could come in handy. Nigel had started particularly early this morning and Emyr could already see the lines of annoyance around the corners of his father's eyes.

An observant servant noticed as well and handed the King a flask from which he took a long grateful draft.

A mental sigh escaped the Prince. It would one day be his duty to listen to men such as this. Might as well get the hang of it now. He pasted his best politician's smile on his face and turned his full attention on the Baron. "Lord Nigel, good to see you again this morning. How are you today? I imagine this arid desert is a far cry from your home in Licea."

Lord Nigel's face turned pink at being addressed directly by both the King and Crown Prince. "Oh yes! It is, Your Highness, but I assure you I am quite well! Nothing like a little adventure to make one appreciate home all the more." His voice was like air being let out of a bag and its thinness grated on both Emyr and his father's nerves, but his last statement rang with reluctant truth. Emyr missed the Royal Palace and the people of Tsifira. He missed the colorful ships in the harbor and the amazing parties hosted by his noble and not-so-noble friends. *Only a month more and I'll be home.*

The never-ending train of Lords, Ladies, servants, and guards rode throughout the day, stopping only to water the horses and eat lunch before moving on. The shadow of Angerona grew larger on the horizon, its black spires cutting a jagged line across the darkening sky. The great Black City filled their vision and Emyr realized that its darkness didn't just come from its reputation for being the most crime-ridden city in Jesimae.

All of the buildings in Angerona were built of a black or deep grey stone that had been brought from overseas more than a thousand years ago. The city was built before Emyr's royal ancestors had even set foot on this continent. No one knew what kind of stone it was because any further deposits were distinctly absent from Jesimae and the Five Kingdoms. Some said the native Elymas people had created it with dark magic, but most people figured they had simply used so much in the building of the city that there was no longer any left. Historians had searched the known world and come up empty handed every time.

When they reached the imposing city gates, the Governor's Herald trumpeted their arrival and Emyr watched a gold and white flag with his family crest run up the tallest tower of the Governor's Palace in the distance, followed by his father's personal flag and his own. The Governor and his party rode out to greet them in person and after a few pleasantries, they rode into the city. The Governor was a non-descript, average-looking man. Emyr could see how the Rogue easily manipulated him; he was almost more deferential to King Besian than Baron Nigel was. Looking at him carefully, Emyr could see the strain behind his eyes though. This was a man who clearly was not cut out for the job of maintaining a city that was insistent upon ruling itself in whatever way it saw fit.

Up close, Emyr could see that there were strange symbols carved into the walls of buildings and the stones of the streets. They reminded him of the markings on the skin of the Elymas healer his father employed. The Elymas people as a whole were frowned upon by high society, but no one could contest that their abilities were extremely useful. He knew they had strict rules about the use of magic nowadays to try and bring the Elymas to heel. The healer, Emmett, had told him that he had been cast out of his clan for wanting to work for the Unchosen (what the Elymas called humans). Emmett had told him that the Elymas resented being feared and having their power limited given that they considered themselves to be Jesimae's First People. He wondered what meaning these symbols held that were so painstakingly carved into every surface in this ancient city. Were they merely for decoration or was there real power within them? Even though he knew many people who had theories, Emyr didn't think there was anyone alive who could tell him the real answer—not even the people who bore the same marks on their skin.

As soon as they were within the city, Emyr felt as though they were immediately enveloped by darkness and Baela nickered at the sudden drop in light and temperature. He placed his hand on her neck gently, stroking her silky mane. "Easy girl, we're almost there." But Emyr was just as wary; the sun had all but disappeared as soon as they had passed through the city gates. The stone seemed to absorb more and more light, the further they went toward the city center, but retained none of the heat.

The main Palace Way was decorated in bright colors and banners in an attempt to make the royal retinue feel welcome, but the stark contrast from the gloomy and imposing buildings merely mocked them.

The streets looked empty. The sound of the horses' hooves rang jarringly in the silence. Even the nobles that normally gossiped like magpies were silent in awe and trepidation. Occasionally, Emyr would catch a glimpse of a boot rounding the corner in an alleyway or a curtain being hastily pushed back into place. Clearly, the people of Angerona were wary of their normally distant ruler and had chosen to stay out of the way rather than risk calling attention to themselves by being one of the few to show their face.

It wasn't until they were almost at the Governor's Palace that Emyr actually spotted someone—well, someone's silhouette. He could see the outline of a tall man with long hair atop one of the roofs backlit against the fading light. There was no way to tell for sure, but Emyr felt sure the man was looking right at him. His sense of dread grew. The gates to the Palace grinding open drew Emyr's focus away from the roof for a brief moment. When he looked back, the man was gone and the Prince was swept along with the rest of the company towards the glowing luxury of the Palace.

Chapter 3
Aedrik

The Royal assemblage was led within the palace's walls to what Aedrik assumed would be a grand and opulent feast. More food would be consumed and wasted tonight than the whole city could put away in a month. He could practically hear his twin's teeth grinding at the thought of it, so he had arranged for some of the food to conveniently "go missing" on its way up to the Great Hall and end up at the nearby orphanage. He was also hoping that the distraction of missing food from the feast would provide some cover for his true goals. It wasn't likely, but he would take any advantage he could get; committing treason was putting him a little on edge.

Slipping off the rooftop and back through the city, he considered tonight's plans. It had to be tonight. There would be a great party, and everyone would be drinking, off their guard. Once the meetings and processions began tomorrow, the security would be much tighter.

Aedrik did think it was interesting that the Prince had spotted him. He wasn't nearly as adept at disguising himself as Ashdan, but no one saw him unless he allowed it. Granted, he hadn't exactly been trying to conceal himself, but most people were too oblivious to spot a dark silhouette on a rooftop. His inside man had spotted him, of course, and given a barely perceptible blink of recognition, but when he'd felt the blue-blood's eyes on him, he'd been forced into a grudging respect for the young man. The other members of the Prince's party had not even glanced in Aedrik's direction. This endeavor was becoming more interesting by the minute. Once again, he wished he didn't have to stay and hold down the fort while his siblings had all the fun. The rush of a good heist was something he lived for, but had had precious few chances to participate in since he'd become Rogue.

He smirked at the empty streets. Some people were out of sight because they were protesting the presence of the King who had largely ignored them for years, but the rest of Angerona new that their Rogue would have something wicked planned for the first night of the Tyrant's stay. They had wisely disappeared behind locked doors and shuttered windows. No one wanted to cross the Rogue when he was out for blood.

The city was strikingly beautiful when it was like this. Sometimes, in a quiet moment, he could reach out with his magic and feel the pulse of the city. Somehow, he could connect with the very stones that held each building together. It was the remnant of an ancient magic that had long since been lost, but he reveled in brushing up against it when there was no one around.

Aedrik kept to the shadows and out of sight. When he reached the Eagle's Nest Inn, he slid in through a secret entrance he'd found as a teenager and materialized at his usual table. The old innkeeper, Ellis, had already set up the table with his usual drink. The old man had an uncanny knack for knowing the moment a table was about to be occupied. As a kid, Aedrik had always been mildly disappointed to find that he could never manage to sneak in without Ellis kicking him out before his butt had even hit a seat. The Eagle's Nest had been operating at the edge of the city in the Lower District for longer than anyone could remember.

Ellis wasn't the original owner, though no one could tell you who was. It was the only building in the Lower District tall enough to see over the wall and therefore, had become a hub of all kinds of information from outside

Angerona—as if having a better sight-line of the rest of the country meant the Nest was privy to more information. Aedrik had seen to it that it became his Court above ground as soon as he'd taken over as the Rogue. His violent, but dimwitted father, Damian, had never realized the advantage the place could afford him during his own reign. His short-sightedness had cost him the throne and his life.

Aedrik passed his drink to the right as the chair next to him scraped the floor. A slight young man with short chocolate brown hair and black eyes perched daintily on the worn wood.

"Hey, sis." Ashdan had never been able to deceive either of her brothers. Their magic was too strongly connected. "Have a drink."

A quicksilver grin crossed the boy's face.

"If you weren't able to recognize my energy, you wouldn't even know it was me."

"Don't pout. It's only cute when you do it as yourself. Too bad for you, my blood runs in your veins. I would know you even if you were a two hundred fifty-pound Elite Guardsman."

Ashdan's nose crinkled in annoyance as she took a drink from his mug. Ellis swept by silently with another three mugs full of good strong ale. He knew Aedrik never drank alone for long.

"No more...personal...errands today?"

The impish face gave him a mischievous smile. "If I ran all my errands today, what would I do tomorrow?" She pushed his tankard back to him and grabbed one for herself.

An amused snort drew their attention to Aedrian who had just arrived and was leaning down to kiss their sister on the cheek. She pushed him away and into the chair next to her where he sat with a chuckle and swiped one of the remaining drinks. He wasn't fooled by her boyish appearance either.

Aedrik ignored their banter in favor of pushing ahead with business. "Everything ready?" His brother reached up and tapped something underneath his shirt. Aedrik saw the string that he'd tied around the Key disappearing under the cloth, and the excitement that had lain dormant all day began to build once more in his chest. A wicked sense of glee bubbled up.

"Good. If all goes as planned, you all will be long gone with the Prince by this time tomorrow and Deorick and I will be bracing ourselves for the onslaught of royal wrath."

"'Bout damn time." The growl came from Aedrik's other side. Deorick straddled the chair backwards, the old wood creaking under his weight. The tankard he pulled from the table was dwarfed by his enormous hand.

"Here, here," they chorused. The few other people in the Nest glanced over at the four men in the corner and quickly away, shifting anxiously. Whatever the Rogue was celebrating, as long as it wasn't their impending deaths, they didn't want to know.

Chapter 4
Aedrian

A couple hours later, the crew split up. Aedrik went outside the Nest to the city gates to prepare for their departure. The other three slid into the shadows—with a little help from Ashdan's magic—and made their way toward the Governor's Palace. It was getting late. The party would be winding down and its attendees heading to their feather beds and silk sheets. That meant it was time to get *their* party started.

They made a quick pit stop at the Vault where they'd had their meeting earlier to gather weapons and essentials. They had found over the years that the abandoned underground fortress proved useful on many fronts. It was where they held their most private meetings, not to mention stored their most valuable items. Early on in Aedrik's reign, they had found a way to spell the Vault so that only those with express permission from Aedrik himself could enter. Initially, Aedrik had wanted to keep the Prince there once he was captured, but Aedrian had pointed out that the King's Elymas mages would be able to track him if he was too close. That was when they'd settled on their mother's mountain home across the country.

Ashdan morphed into a distinguished-looking middle-aged noblewoman. Carrying her goody basket and accompanied by two heavily armed men, she appeared to be out for a nighttime stroll with her two bodyguards. Considering people generally didn't stroll around Angerona at night, Aedrian reminded her to be careful and give a little extra emphasis to the stealth part of their glamour.

The sharp, hot coastal wind tugged at Aedrian's long hair like fingers trying to pull him back. He reached up and tied it back while placing his feet carefully on stones worn smooth from hundreds of years of feet, hooves, and wheels passing over them. His eyes flicked toward every flash of movement, every deep shadow. As they walked, he rested one hand on the sword at his waist and loosened a dagger from its sheath with the other.

When they reached the Servant's Gate, a guard of medium height and build peered down at them from the parapet. His average and forgettable appearance was one of the reasons he was so useful tonight. A breeze lifted the hairs off the backs of their necks as they waited for him to open the small door within the massive gate. Aedrian signaled to Ashdan to drop the stealth glamour, but not their disguises, knowing that any noblewoman caught wondering palace grounds after a grand party would hardly be found at fault whereas one of the Rogue's people would be caught and hanged. They stayed on the edges of the pools of lantern light until they reached the stables.

He and Ashdan turned to Deorick who was looking at them sternly. "If you aren't back in six minutes, I'm coming in after you. Then at least I'll have another four to get you out." Ashdan patted Deorick on the shoulder, or rather, the elbow since that was as high as she could reach.

"Don't worry, *Papa*," she chided, "We'll be back with His Royal Highness before you have the chance to say, 'Don't get caught.' Again, that is." His scowl said he didn't believe them, but he nodded and headed into the stable to ready the horses. Both Aedrian and Ashdan were suddenly glad they weren't stable boys tonight. Those poor lads would wake up with nasty headaches and probably lose their jobs—at best.

"He seems edgier than usual."

"Ashdan, we're committing high treason. Why wouldn't he be edgy?"

"No, I-"

She cut off and pushed him against the wall, peering around the corner. He wanted to shove her now fat, wrinkled hand away from his chest in disgust, but managed a slightly less dramatic flick instead. She glared at him then went back to watching the courtyard. A few seconds later, she signaled the all clear and sprinted across the expanse toward the round wall of the Keep. Aedrian followed at a more cautious pace, not having actually seen whether the coast was clear and rolling his eyes at her eagerness.

They walked around the edge of the building until they were between it and a six-foot tall garden hedge. Behind them, the moonless garden maze backed up to a small gazebo that sat on the edge of the cliffs. Aedrian could see himself thoroughly enjoying that spot in another life. For tonight, though, he had a mission, and he would not —could not— fail.

He pulled the Skeleton Key from under his shirt. Neither of them doubted Aedrik's abilities for a second, but they were still somewhat incredulous of the artifact's power. He set the flat bottom of the Key against the cold grey brick and reached within himself for his power. According to Aedrik, all it would take was a small push of magic and the Key would start working. He set the spiral on top to its highest setting and released his power. Their faces glowed briefly blue in the light from the magically charged markings on his skin and...

...their brother had simply outdone himself.

The Key attached itself to the wall and started to unravel, forming a larger and larger octagon from the pieces that had formed its spiral. The only sound was the wind through the hedges behind them, but dim light glowed from the edges of a hole that had begun to grow in the brick wall. When the hole stopped growing, Ashdan and Aedrian stood in front of a dimly pulsing doorway. It looked as if the primordial chaos of creation had melted the stone wall, leaving an opening large enough for them to pass through. Phase one of the plan was officially in motion.

Inside, they could see the contents of a storeroom. They would be entering on the servants' level of the Keep and would work their way up to Prince Emyr from there. They exchanged a brief glance, making a mental note to *never* tell Aedrik they were impressed, and entered the building.

Now there was only darkness and the waiting breath of silence and anticipation.

Chapter 5
Ashdan

The storeroom was blacker than the stone it was built from, but being half Elymas, the siblings had better than average night vision and could pick their way silently through the detritus. At the far door, they paused briefly—now came the hard part. Ashdan tapped the timepiece hanging from her glamour's vest pocket—five minutes left.

The markings on her hand would have flared the briefest blue when she touched the knob of the door had she not been currently wearing the form of another person. This time, there was no awe-inspiring display of innovative magic, only a quiet click and they were led out into a dimly lit hallway. They made their way along the far wall, edging to the door at the end on their right—the servant's stair.

Ashdan quickly changed the glamour in case they were spotted by anyone. Now she looked like a simple scullery maid and he an off-duty guardsman. If they were spotted, people would just assume they were a couple trying to find some "alone time." She decided she wouldn't tell Aedrian that part, knowing he would probably get grossed out if people thought that of him and his sister.

Flight after flight of stairs, they climbed. They passed one petite maid on her way down to her bedroom, but she was so tired, she gave them the barest of nods and continued on her way. Ashdan doubted she'd even seen their faces; the poor girl's eyes were half closed. Not that it mattered. Since she'd cast a glamour, no one had a chance of recognizing them unless they were actively using a counter spell. There were many wards within the Palace walls, but a revelation spell was not one of them. Ashdan suspected that was because the rich and entitled were always paying ridiculous amounts for appearance altering spells. For once, the vanity and arrogance of the nobles who lived in Angerona was working in their favor.

They reached the bend before the fifth-floor landing. She stopped briefly and pushed her shoulders back, shaking out her hair. She figured Aedrian would take that as a signal to prepare himself. He put his right hand on his hip at the hilt of a hidden knife and his left on the same hip at the pommel of his sword. Ashdan flashed an excited grin over her shoulder at him before continuing around the corner. She knew he sometimes wondered if his siblings derived a little too much pleasure from causing mischief. He was probably right.

One of the Prince's guards, Barrett, was resting on a palette outside the door. His big frame barely fit the cushioned pad. Neither sibling envied him his job at this moment except for the access it afforded to the Prince. She thought he might be sleeping, but when she took another step forward, his eyes snapped open—dark pools filled with higher-than-average intelligence and sharp wariness. When he spotted them, he sat up, a hand on his unsheathed sword hilt.

"What business have you outside the Prince's door?" he growled.

Ashdan flashed two newly placed dimples at the rugged warrior and let her hair fall behind her shoulder, exposing a long, graceful neck.

"I thought you might be hungry. You and your friend had to work all night while the Prince was wined and dined. I know you got a few scraps in the kitchen a while ago, but that can't possibly have been enough; especially for a man as big as you." She could practically hear her brother gagging behind her when she ran her eyes over the guard in a manner that made her meaning of "big" clear.

She gave him a sly wink and sat her pert bottom right next to him on the landing. With another endearing smile, she offered him her basket. He peaked inside and when he caught a whiff of the goods packed in there, his eyes nearly rolled back in his head. The smell emitting from the basket was heavenly—giving a lie to what lay within.

"Why did you need a guard to bring me sweets?"

"Oh him? That's just my...friend." The way she said the last word didn't leave much open for interpretation. Aedrian covered up an indignant scoff by clearing his throat loudly.

"He insisted on coming with me. Said it wasn't safe for a girl to wander around at night, even in a well-defended castle!" She widened her eyes comically on the last statement.

Barrett gave her an indulgent grin, but made no move to take the basket. "Your friend is probably right, little one." Ashdan could see that Aedrian had been counting the minutes in his head. If her feminine charms didn't work soon, both were prepared to subdue him forcefully, but that would cause a lot of disruption and neither of them particularly wanted to hurt anyone who didn't have to get involved.

They needn't have worried though because as soon as Barrett started to make his excuses and dismiss them, Ashdan pulled a small cookie from the basket and bit into it. The Elite Guardsman's eyes locked on her lips, and she knew she had him. Then she decided to share in the fun and turned to offer Aedrian the rest. He faked a smile and placed the sweet concoction on his tongue. When he found it to be quite delicious, he didn't have to fake his groan of delight.

Despite the worry she knew he was feeling that she'd just drugged or killed them both with her tentative poisoning skills, Aedrian trusted her and was aware that to second guess her at this moment would be the death of both of them. He held his tongue and grinned back down at her. It was all the encouragement the guard needed.

He peered into the basket again and said hungrily, "Let's see what else you got here."

Chapter 6
Emyr

Emyr woke to soft voices out on the servants' stair. He knew Barrett was out there, but when he looked across the room, Calloway was dozing on a cot by the fire. Who was Barrett talking to then? After a minute or two, the voices stopped and Emyr lay back again, sinking into the mountain of down pillows behind his head. Whoever Barrett had been speaking with must have left. He glanced at the clock and sighed—two minutes until the second hour of the morning. The nervous feeling that had been haunting him all day was still there, but he felt if he could just make it to sunrise things would be okay.

Just then, Calloway stirred on his cot, rolled over, and sat up facing Emyr. The dark eyes blinked sleepily at him before glancing at the clock and coming fully awake.

"Can't sleep, my Prince?" The man's sharp eyes did not miss the worry etched into Emyr's tired face. Emyr shook his head.

"I know something that might help. It should have been delivered to Barrett by now." He got up and walked to the servants' door. *That explains who was out there just a few seconds ago,* Emyr thought. Silently, Calloway slid through the door and reappeared seconds later with a basket from which came the most heavenly smells.

"Are those...?"

"Your favorites? Just like they make in the Capital? These are better."

"You guys really do think of everything," Emyr mumbled with a sleepy smile. The pastries looked decadent and freshly baked. Emyr was a very fit individual, but once in a while, he gave in to the craving and had something unhealthy. Most nobles didn't understand why their Crown Prince restricted what he ate. Their lives were filled with whatever shallow pleasures they could get their hands on—if they wanted the richest most delicious foods the kingdom had to offer, they got them. They also died at alarmingly young ages and fell out of fighting condition before they had even hit their prime. Emyr had realized some time ago, however, that despite the short-term satisfaction rich food gave him, eating it all the time left him feeling ill and sluggish. Given the battles his father was fond of waging against neighboring countries, a sluggish day could mean the difference between life and death for the Crown Prince.

But tonight was different. It had been a long, taxing day—what with half the day spent riding towards the city from the desert and the other half rubbing elbows with people trying to kiss his father's ass. Emyr felt he deserved the treat Calloway had put in front of him, so he raised the small pastry, "Cheers," and popped the whole thing into his mouth. Oh gods. Calloway was right. These were even better than the ones he got at home. There was something slightly different about the taste...As the sweet chocolatey goodness filled his senses, Emyr no longer felt on edge or cared about anything else. A sudden comfort streamed through his exhausted limbs. It was as if the exertions of the day had all tumbled in at once and his body grew heavy with fatigue.

He reached into the basket and pulled out another, popping it into his mouth as he had the first. He waved away Calloway's offer of anything else and sank back into his pillows. Nothing had ever felt so utterly serene as this room and this bed. His eyes pulled themselves shut of their own accord and the last thing he heard before he passed out was the servant's door opening once more and several sets of footsteps approaching his bed...

Chapter 7
Ashdan

Ashdan listened to her brother shifting the weight of the Prince on his shoulder; she didn't envy him the job of carrying that burden. Aedrian was as strong as they came, but the Prince was no fainting nobleman—he seemed to be nothing but solid muscle. *What? A girl notices these things,* she argued when the sensible half of her brain scolded. They had waited a few precious seconds while Calloway had tied Barrett to the solid oak bed frame. The poor man would wake from his drug induced slumber and hate himself for falling for her tricks. She didn't think it would be any consolation that he hadn't really stood a chance. They would have taken him out of the equation one way or another; this way was so much more pleasant. Everyone was still alive and unharmed.

After Barrett had crumbled under Ashdan's influence and taken the pastry, it had been easy to get in. In the few more seconds it had taken Calloway and Aedrian to roll the Prince into one of the rugs lying on the floor she took the time to send a quick update message to Deorick. She felt the magic fill her and reveled in the brief euphoric feeling. She quickly let him know that they had the Prince and were on their way out. When she felt the affirmative push in response, she nodded to the other two and they headed out.

Now, the three newly glamoured companions hurried with their tightly wrapped bundle back into the dimly lit storage closet where the miraculous octagonal doorway still glinted expectantly at the far end. Because they had bought themselves a few extra minutes with the message to Deorick, they had taken more care on the way down to remain unseen, but their time with the portal would soon run out. The edges had already begun to waver ominously. Ashdan was practically sprinting toward it through the mountains of crates and sacks of flour. She was watching the portal's dim outline on the opposite wall and knew that they had thirty seconds—tops—to get out before the doorway would disappear, leaving them to find another, less assured way out.

To be honest, when she had scoffed at Deorick's doubt over their ability to complete the mission within the time constraints, she hadn't been one hundred percent confident, but she would never have admitted that to his face. Now she knew she had underestimated the Prince's trust in Calloway. Without it, they would have been trapped, trying to forcibly subdue the Prince who happened to be one of the Realm's most renowned warriors.

The siblings had grown up with Calloway and hadn't thought twice of asking him to be party to their plans. She almost felt bad that she hadn't had faith in him, but he *had* been away for quite some time. Of course, he had made sure that they took a blood oath stating that the Prince would come to no harm, but since Emyr was not actually the siblings' target, they'd had no problem doing so. Besides, all three knew that harming the Prince would be a huge detriment to the country, which despite popular belief, they *were* trying to help. Everyone knew Emyr would make an excellent King someday. He was beloved by his subjects across the Kingdom.

So it was that three shadows darted back through the portal—with much tripping and cursing from the fully human one in the rear—just as it flickered into nothing. Not a single trace was left of the opening, only solid stone where it had been before. The Key fell to the soft grass at the foot of the Keep. Ashdan could tell Calloway was trying to hide his amazement at Aedrik's handiwork, but he was hardly succeeding. She stopped and picked up the small ornate octagon that was responsible for the amazing feat they had just witnessed and handed it back to Aedrian for safe keeping. When it came to spell creation, there could no longer be any doubt, Aedrik was the most skilled of the three siblings.

They crept into the stables where Deorick was waiting with four already saddled horses, including the Prince's mare, Baela. Aedrik had been sure to tell him what the horse looked like after catching sight of the Prince earlier that day. It would make the journey easier for all of them if at least one horse knew its rider. Since Deorick would only be going with them as far as the city gates, Aedrian swung the Prince over the horse's back and climbed up behind the unconscious man. Baela seemed to be a little uncomfortable with the strange passenger at first, but no animal had ever been able to resist Aedrian for long. She went quiet after he stroked her mane a few times while murmuring softly into her ear. Ashdan had always wondered what he said to calm animals down like that, but she knew he would never tell.

Their small crew hurried as silently as possible out of the stables. As she shut and locked the stable doors behind them, Ashdan noticed a pair of feet sticking out from a small pile of hay next to the door. She walked over to it, ignoring her brother's hiss to "get moving." A cold feeling settled within her rib cage as she approached the battered boot-covered feet. She gently brushed the hay from the unconscious man's face. Not a man. Barely even a teenager. The lankiness of youth made his body look too big for his childish features. And not unconscious. Dead. She turned away and found Deorick standing right behind her, his eyes boring into hers. In that moment she knew exactly what had happened. Deorick had killed the boy.

Anger, red hot, melted the ice within her. She'd known something was off with Deorick and still couldn't figure out why he would have done it. This boy didn't deserve to die. That wasn't the point of this mission. He'd been innocent. But now she itched to get back to Aedrik and warn him of their friend's instability.

When Ashdan climbed back onto her horse after gently closing the boy's eyes, she could feel Deorick's eyes still on her. She looked up and knew that hers were blazing with anger. Nothing to do about it now, they had to get off the Palace grounds before they were caught.

The same person who'd let them in, let them back out without question even though they all looked completely different. Ashdan saw Aedrian toss something up to the man before they rode away; presumably, a hefty payment for his services. No point in expecting loyalty if you weren't going to return the favor. That bag of coins would probably feed the man's family for a year. Or fund their escape to a new city. *She* wouldn't want to stick around once the Guardsmen found out the kidnappers had entered through the Servant's Gate. She hoped they got away safely.

They rode through the city, avoiding the main roadways. Now that they were out of the Palace, an even greater sense of urgency set in. They wanted to be far from the city by the time the Prince woke up. The trip back to the Lower District was easy enough and they reached the Nest without incident, greeting Aedrik quietly.

"He's in there?" asked their hard-eyed brother, pointing to the rolled-up carpet on the regal horse's back.

"Nice and snug," Aedrian responded, patting the part of the rug Ashdan assumed was the Prince's ass. She choked back a laugh as Aedrik rolled his eyes. The mood was charged with nervous energy, and they cracked several jokes as they recounted their escape to Aedrik in an attempt to release the tension. Still snickering, they slid off their horses and congregated for a final meeting, ignoring the sounds coming from inside the Nest.

Even at this hour, the Nest was never empty, but it would only be filled with people who were loyal to the Rogue—it being his Court and all. Nevertheless, they chose to remain in the empty darkness outside the building's warm glow. A swift conversation forged from whispers occurred where they stood, having finally sobered sufficiently to match the occasion. Ashdan decided to send Aedrik a message privately to tell him about the dead boy. She would be away from Deorick soon, but she didn't want to leave Aedrik alone with someone so volatile. If the older man was becoming unreliable, Aedrik needed to be on his guard. This was a crucial time for all of them.

They finished their discussion and gathered their supplies: tents, food, water, and weapons for the journey. Aedrik disappeared into the Nest, presumably to resolve whatever dispute had been growing louder as they'd stood outside. Within seconds, the noise abated and they all knew whatever had happened would no longer be an issue. Deorick disappeared into the shadows, Ashdan squinting after him in worry. As soon as they were outside the city gates, she would call to Aedrik as she had to Deorick earlier and tell him of her concerns.

When they had everything ready to go, Ashdan, Aedrian, Calloway, and the unconscious Prince Emyr began to make their way on horseback to the city gates, Aedrian securing the Prince before mounting the horse Deorick had climbed off of moments earlier.

They were almost to the gates when something whistled past Aedrian's right ear and embedded itself in the alley wall beyond. They all quickly scrambled off their horses and pulled out weapons. Calloway pulled the Prince/rug down and stood guard over him with his back against the alley wall. Aedrian and Ashdan put their backs to him and stood on high alert.

"That was a knife," breathed Aedrian.

"Ya think?" Ashdan shifted on the balls of her feet, ready for a fight. She saw something moving out of the corner of her eye. No alarm had been raised at the Palace, so it wasn't anyone trying to rescue the Prince. Besides, the Elite Guardsmen—the Royal family's personal guard—used swords and bows and arrows. She doubted any of them could throw a knife as well as her or her siblings. The knife had been a good throw, but not accurate enough. The thrower was quite possibly a member of the Court of the Rogue, in which case, they were a traitor and needed to be taken down immediately and without mercy.

Speaking of...

A rushing sound signaled the entrance of several masked figures into the alley way. An ambush! But by whom? Who had known where they would be at this exact moment in time? She and Aedrian fought off the first two easily enough; it was an unwritten rule in a fight to always send in the weakest first. This time, Ashdan had no qualms about slitting the man's throat. The knife she pulled from her wrist sheath cut through his neck like butter. She may have been horrified that Deorick had killed an innocent child, but anyone who attacked her or her family put themselves at her mercy and when it came to protecting herself and her big brothers, she had none.

Masked fighters dashed in from all sides, two charging toward Ashdan, two to her brother, and two to Calloway. Evidently, this attack had been well-coordinated by someone who had known Calloway would be with them. Ashdan executed a vicious round-house kick to the face of the guy coming at her from the left. He landed with a sickening sound—impaled on the spikes of the iron fence behind him. She whirled around, but wasn't fast enough to block the blow from her other opponent. She stumbled back, but only for an instant.

There was something about this man that seemed familiar, but she was having a hard time placing it as they danced back and forth, trading blows. They fought hand-to-hand in earnest, but this fellow played dirty. He was matching Ashdan's basic skills relatively easily, so she knew it was time to break out a few of her deadlier tricks. She managed to detach herself momentarily and activated her claws. Ten small blades attached to the wrist sheaths she had pulled the first knife from—one for each finger—sprang from their hiding place, razor sharp. She spread them out and went to engage her enemy again, but he was gone. She could just spot him sprinting around a corner at the far end of the alley. He didn't spare a single glance for his impaled comrade as he rushed past.

Ignoring the wretched feeling that his green eyes had given her, she went to help her brother. He was still entangled with the other two masked men, his preferred weapons being two longer, slightly curved daggers that flashed through the darkness like small fires. He was holding his own, but both men were good enough fighters to keep coming at him, the big one especially. Again, something about this man left her unsettled.

Ashdan jumped on the back of the smaller of the two. Not the most sophisticated fighting style, but hey, when your enemy fought dirty, sometimes you needed to improvise. She wrapped her legs high around his chest, restricting his ability to breathe, and grabbed his head in a headlock with one arm. One arm wasn't going to kill him, but it would buy her all the time she needed. She flexed her claws and slashed savagely across the part of his throat exposed when she wrenched his head back.

Man down.

Ashdan dropped gracefully to her toes as the dead man sank to the ground in a heap and turned to help Aedrian take on the final opponent. She needn't have worried. Not having to fight two men at once, meant that Aedrian's considerable skill was solely focused on his remaining adversary. As soon as the man realized he was surrounded by the two of them and alone, he shoved Aedrian hard and disengaged, only turning to look back one final time.

Aedrian and Ashdan normally wouldn't have let potential assassins go without at least unmasking them so they could find them later, but their most pressing concern was for the Prince and that final glance back had told them everything they needed to know. It even helped Ashdan place the horrible feeling she'd gotten from the other man who had fled. The shock began to set in as she recalled the familiar features of the first man who had turned tail so quickly.

Kilian. Those muddy green eyes were recognizable even behind a mask. Normally, the siblings would be brainstorming how the evil little malfunction had even found out what they were doing, but their final opponent had given them that answer—Deorick. The eyes behind Aedrian's large opponent's mask were nearly as familiar to them as their own. Their longtime friend, who had been a part of their family for longer than any of them could remember, was the one who had betrayed them. Ashdan had known something was off, but she never would have expected this.

Aedrian looked at his sister, his face pale. His expression seemed to articulate the agony of betrayal that words could not. "He's served our family since before we were born. He helped Aedrik take the throne from Father! Why—" Color flooded swiftly back into his cheeks along with the anger and his knuckles had turned white where he gripped the handles of his beloved daggers. His chest and glyphs, now exposed due to damage to his clothes from the fight, heaved and blue sparks crackled along his glyphs in response to his heightened emotions. His eyes glowed in their light. Ashdan simply shook where she stood, hurt and anger preventing her from speaking about it just yet. To see Aedrian lose control like that was a rare enough thing to witness and she knew he was deeply wounded by this betrayal.

She turned to Calloway who had somehow managed to hold on to all of the horses and guard the still unconscious and quietly sleeping Prince. She wasn't at all surprised to find three more dead men littering the ground near him. The man didn't have a single morsel of magic within in him, but he could probably kick all their asses in a fair fight. She was just glad he was on their side instead of reporting them to the Guard who still had yet to raise an alarm at the Palace.

Calloway caught her looking at him. "They came from the roof." She nodded and took her still fuming brother's hand. "We need to tell Aedrik and then we need to go. The sun will be rising in a couple hours. I don't want to still be in view of the city when they discover the Prince is missing."

I knew I should have warned Aedrik about him, she thought in frustration.

Calloway spoke up again. "It might be better if you and I stay, Aedrian. Leaving Aedrik alone to face this onslaught..."

Aedrian nodded his head, "He would be dead by morning. Ashdan, I know you're more than capable of getting Emyr to Sonneillon. Between your disguises and claws, he'll be safe. Just be careful. He's a crafty one, our Prince."

She started to protest, but Calloway was nodding in agreement. He took his duty to the Prince very seriously. If he trusted Ashdan to protect him, then maybe Aedrian was right.

Aedrian continued, "Besides, the fewer people traveling on open road, the less of a target you'll be. Though I have to say, I am kind of envious of you, getting to spend all that alone time with the Prince," he finished with a half-hearted attempt at humor.

Ashdan smacked her brother's arm. Calloway slapped the back of his head. "Don't be crude. That man's going to be King someday."

Their reactions only spurred him on.

"Aye, but right now he makes a very handsome rug." He jumped out of the way before Calloway or Ashdan could smack him again and continued, changing the subject.

"It's set then. Cal, let's release the extra horses and go find Aedrik. Little sis," and here his eyes and tone got suddenly very serious, "good luck." She nodded, knowing all the things he was trying to say with those two words. This wasn't what they had planned, but circumstances called for it. She would die before she left Aedrik to face the dangers of this ultimate treachery alone. The assassination attempts and territorial skirmishes had gotten bad and Kilian was a nuisance, but now it was of the utmost importance that her brothers hunt down Deorick and get an explanation. It would have taken some immense persuading to sway the loyalty of a man who had protected them their whole lives. Whoever had been able to do that was their biggest threat.

As she turned away to situate the Prince on his horse once more, she noticed it.

"Aed—"

"Yeah?"

"Where's the Skeleton Key?"

He looked down at his chest where he'd hung the Key after she'd handed it back to him. Blue sparks started coming off his fingers and glyphs again.

"Damn him!" When Deorick had shoved Aedrian to disengage from the fight, he had ripped Aedrian's shirt and, in the process, stolen the Key.

"We'll find him, Aedrian." Calloway's voice was soothing as he placed a firm hand on Aedrian's neck. "We'll find him *and* Kilian and then we'll make those sons of bitches pay for what they've done to all of us."

Aedrian seemed able to find the strength to calm himself in Calloway's eyes. Their gazes remained locked for a second longer before Calloway dropped his hand and helped Ashdan with the Prince. Ashdan arched an eyebrow at him as they unrolled the Prince from the rug. Was he blushing? *They would probably be great together,* she thought.

Maybe it was because her mind had gone down a romantic and slightly lecherous road, but once the Prince was fully unrolled from the rug, she caught her breath a little. No wonder he was the darling of Jesimae and several realms beyond, the man was flawless. Now it was Aedrian's turn to punch *her* in the arm for staring lustfully.

"Behave." He growled in her ear. She rolled her eyes.

Calloway lifted the Prince easily and set him astride the mare, whose name Aedrian had learned upon speaking with her was Baela. Aedrian stepped forward, twining a small weed he'd plucked from the ground around his fingers. With their glamours gone, his glyphs glowed as the weed expanded and grew until it had become large enough to tie around the Prince's hands. Aedrian lashed him to the front of the saddle as much for his safety as to keep him prisoner. He repeated the process two more times and bound both feet to the stirrups. Now the Prince would not fall off his horse while still unconscious, but he would also not escape when he eventually woke up. Aedrian sometimes complained that his talent with plants and animals was lame, but Ashdan thought it was magnificent. She loved to watch him work.

"All set, Ash," Calloway said after checking the bindings and saddle once more.

"Fly, little sister, as fast as you can." Aedrian placed a kiss on his sister's auburn head. For once, she wore her true face when she turned a concerned smile up at him. She didn't bother with another glamour yet because she had come to terms with the fact that Calloway had known her as a child and killing him for seeing her true face would be redundant.

She mounted her horse with a nimble leap and glanced back one more time. Aedrian and Calloway had already disappeared into the blackness of the Angeronian streets. She made the sign for luck, kissing the top joint of her right thumb, and urged the two horses forward, praying to all the gods to keep her brothers and old friend safe.

Chapter 8

Emyr

Emyr woke with his head pounding, feeling like he was about to throw up. Just kidding, not about to. The dinner and sweets he'd eaten the night before fell to the hard earth below him in a violent burst, narrowly avoiding Baela's pristine mane. She snorted indignantly. He raised his hand to wipe his mouth. Or, at least, he tried to. *Wait, what?*

Opening his eyes further, he realized his hands were strapped to the pommel of his saddle with some kind of—plant? *What in all the realms of darkness? Wait.* Why was he in his saddle? He forced himself to sit up straight and take in his surroundings, every muscle protesting. All he saw for miles were jagged outcroppings of rock. When he swiveled around to see behind him, there was nothing but the same. He was back in the desert they'd ridden through yesterday. He couldn't help the groan of agony that slipped through his lips. He had come to hate this part of Jesimae more than any other he had ever visited.

To his left, a voice sighed, "Well, at least you didn't get sick all over your horse. She probably wouldn't have appreciated that."

She wouldn't have, but he glared at the plump woman on the horse next to him anyway.

"Who are you? Where are you taking me?" At least, that's what he meant to come out. His throat was so dry though, the only sound that came out was a desperate rasp. It didn't help that his mouth now tasted like bile. The woman pushed the cloth she'd wrapped around her raven hair back with one hand as she reached into her saddlebags with the other. He tensed, but all she pulled out was a water skin. She took a drink from it first, then held the opening to his cracked lips, pulling her horse closer to his. He remained wary, but drank the water anyway. Whatever the situation, he still had to survive until he got back home. Water first, then escape.

"You can relax. I'm not going to hurt you. I'll even let you go when I have what I need."

His voice returned, Emyr tried again, "Who are you? Where are you taking me? What do you want?"

"Can't tell you. To all three." She slipped the water skin back into the bag near her right leg. He mourned its disappearance acutely, but he took the opportunity to study her. She looked like one of the nomadic people that traveled the desert in Jesimae. They had been infamously branded as robbers and thieves, but he couldn't recall any instances where they went within castle walls to kidnap someone. He was puzzled by the woman, to say the least.

He didn't see any of the telltale black glyphs that they usually had, but the nomads were descended from—if not directly of—the Elymas people. Chances were, she was hiding her markings because most people in Jesimae reacted to "tatties" with fear and revulsion—except when they found use for them, of course. Her voice was dry and deep with a slight accent that recalled a life spent travelling under the scorching sun. Her eyes, though jet black, sparkled with humor and mischief as she gazed back at him.

"Listen, you probably already know this, but I can pay you a great deal of money if you promise to release me unharmed. In return, I can promise to not seek retribution." He hoped she did not sense the lie in his voice, but figured she wasn't stupid enough to fall for that. Emyr wasn't in the habit of underestimating his enemy, but it never hurt to try the simplest solution first. His suspicions were confirmed when she merely gave him a half smile and tucked a stray lock of hair under her head covering.

"You will be released unharmed—" his head snapped up, but she continued, "—when I get what I need." And that was that. She would speak no further.

They rode for several hours more before the sun began to set. By his best estimate, Emyr believed they were heading Northeast—out of the desert and toward the rivers and mountains—farther away from his home and Angerona with every step. By the time she called a halt, he could still see nothing but jagged rock and cracked earth ahead and behind him. It would most likely be another day or two before they reached the edge of the desert. He hoped to be long gone before then.

The woman looked more agile than he had first thought when she hopped down from her horse and landed gracefully. She guided them to a large outcropping of rock that would shield them from the worst of the wind and nighttime cold. It was a natural shelter that looked as if it had been used by many a wandering traveler as a temporary resting place. There was a small weathered wooden post that she tied the horses' leads to. Then she approached him. He glared down at her, having decided to take a wait-and-see approach. For now, he felt confident she wouldn't hurt him. She seemed to need him for something. Until he found a way to escape, that would work in his favor.

She hovered over one of his bound feet and he tried to see what she was doing, but his vision was obscured by her scarf and abundant hair. When she moved away, however, the plant-rope that had been binding him slithered off into her hand as if it had never been tied to him at all. She repeated the process with his other foot and waved one hand briefly over his own.

"Dismount."

He tested the bindings around his wrists. His hands had been detached from the saddle, but were still bound together. He thought about refusing her request, but they had been riding all day. He was hungry and tired and figured if she meant to keep him safe, she probably wouldn't poison him with dinner.

He pulled one leg over the side of his horse and nearly fell to the ground. He hadn't realized just how sore he would be. Her firm hands gripped his upper arms and steadied him until he was back on his feet. Then she directed him to the far side of an indent in the ground under the outcropping which he assumed was used to build fires. He knew he was taking a lot on faith, but what choice did he have? Until he could further assess his situation, it was best to play her games.

As soon as Emyr was seated, he felt a rope slither around his ankles once more. He sighed. No. This woman wasn't stupid. But then again, neither was he. He just had to wait for the right moment. Then he would be able to overtake her, bind her as she had bound him, and return home to seek justice. He was, after all, much larger than her petite frame. He didn't have his sword—though he thought he might have glimpsed it in her bags—but maybe the knife in his right boot…

She smiled as though she could sense what he was thinking. She seemed to find it amusing that he thought he could escape from her. And maybe it was. She leaned over and reached into his boot to unerringly pull out the small knife. Well. He had learned a few things in that moment. First, she was more observant than most people he encountered ever were.

Second, she was heavily armed.

When she leaned over, Emyr caught the impression of thin knives sheathed beneath her clothing. He decided he would simply have to watch her even more carefully as the night wore on.

Third, she had not disarmed him completely when she'd first taken him hostage. If she had known about the knife as her actions seemed to indicate, why had she left it in his boot until now? Why had she stopped to even put his boots on? He couldn't help but think she was testing him.

She rummaged in her saddlebags until she found a peat block which she placed in the bottom of the fire pit. She lit the block with some matches, no magic, and set about making dinner. Emyr watched silently and began to hatch a plan.

Chapter 9
Aedrian

Aedrian watched the emotions pass over his twin's face as he and Calloway regaled him with tales of recent events. Aedrik was not an easy person for most people to read, but to Aedrian, it was as if he was looking in a mirror. First, shock, then dismay, then confusion, then rage poured over his angular features. Aedrian glanced at Calloway. The normally stoic man looked completely pissed off. Having grown up with them, Cal knew Deorick almost as well as they did. The thought that he was working for or with their enemy, Kilian, was a blow that none of them were yet able to comprehend.

"And Ashdan?"

"She's fine. We sent her to carry on with the Prince. She's the most capable out of all of us of getting him to Sonneillon unharmed."

"True. Well, gents, we've got work to do. Oh, and Cal? Seeing as I'll need someone to fill a suddenly vacant position and you're not likely to be going back to the Guard anytime soon, you've been promoted."

A grin split the blonde man's face—there, then gone.

As Aedrik slipped back into the darkness from whence he came, Aedrian and Calloway made their way across the city to the Dregs, a pub in the worst slum of the city where Kilian and his lackeys had decided to make camp. The brothers were always up for some healthy competition to their authority, but instead of challenging them outright, Kilian had been evading their knives, slinking back into the shadows whenever they turned to fight.

Thinking about that slime ball always made Aedrian want to spit. Now they would have to actually speak to him. The taste in his mouth worsened and this time he actually did spit. Whomever Deorick was working for had apparently thought it a good idea to bring Kilian in on the ambush. Aedrian vowed to disabuse them of their delusions.

To Aedrian's right Calloway was also lost deep in thought. The sharp lines of his face cast shadows and hollowed his cheeks in the dim light. Fire flickered in the depths of his coal-black eyes. He had as much cause to fight Kilian and Deorick as Aedrian and his siblings did. Calloway had been part of the initial takeover of the Court of the Western Rogue several years back. The battles after Aedrik defeated Damian had been long and bloody, but finally, he, Aedrian, Ashdan, and their inner circle had ended up in charge.

When the brothers finally assured him their coup had been successful, Calloway had followed Aedrik's advice and worked his way into the ranks of the Royal family's personal guard. As an Elite Guardsman, Calloway could provide them information from the inside that they never would've obtained otherwise. Aedrian felt a shiver that had nothing to do with fear or cold run through him when their eyes met. Needless to say, there were many reasons he was grateful for Cal's return.

He looked away quickly, having been caught staring. Old crushes never did seem to fade, did they?

Their trek took them away from the Nest, but not any closer to the center of the city. In fact, they ended up circling the perimeter until they were in the South end—the original Thieves' Quarter. The farther away from the main thoroughfare they went, the worse the neighborhoods got, but to the two men this was closer and closer to home.

Aedrian remembered running through the muddy streets with no shoes chasing after his twin and younger sister. The constant danger of being the Rogue's children had helped them hone their fighting skills and magic more quickly than most. Among the trash heaps and middens of Angerona's slums, the siblings and Calloway had been forged into the creatures of deep ambition and fierce loyalty they were today.

And then there was Deorick. He had followed them like a shadow on their father's orders, pulling them out of the worst scrapes.

In this part of town, the people weren't as well hidden as elsewhere in the city. They knew that they were well out of the way of whatever business the Rogue would be conducting while the King was in town, so the pubs and occasional brothel they passed were full and vibrant.

The sounds of laughter, music, and glasses clinking spilled out of open doorways and onto the damp and moss-covered cobblestones. No, these people would not halt their lives for intrigue and treason. They had enough to worry about with keeping their families clothed and fed. They would squeeze out of this life whatever pleasures they could afford and a few they couldn't. Aedrian felt a sudden longing for that simpler life he'd never been allowed to enjoy.

It was the people's wariness of Aedrik and Aedrian's talent for mischief that meant despite the revelry within, not a soul could be spotted wandering the actual streets. The two men made their way to their final destination without a word. It was moments like this that Aedrian wished his sister wasn't miles away and counting. By now she would have thrown a stronger glamour over them than any he could muster, and they could have waltzed in and had dinner with Kilian without him ever catching wise.

With things as they stood, however, they would be forced to use the dim lighting of the dingy pub in their favor. Luckily, for them, this was not the kind of place that spent a lot of money on upkeep. Many of the places where torches would have flickered along the walls held only empty scars as a reminder of what had been pulled down by age or various tavern brawls.

Aedrian gestured for Calloway to enter the place, while he would stick to the shadows outside the windows and listen in. Calloway had been gone for over ten years, long before Kilian's time. Hardly anyone was bound to recognize him. People didn't last long in Angerona. They either fled back from whence they came or were killed. Aedrian's face, however, was so well known that he'd probably be run through on sight.

Cal nodded to him one last time before stepping into the pub. For now, they were fact-finding only; they needed to gather more information before they could confront Kilian. Aedrian shook his head, still slightly in disbelief at the situation they found themselves in.

Well, here goes nothing.

The door to the Dregs shut tightly behind his friend and he was left in the darkness alone with only his listening spell to keep him company.

Chapter 10
Calloway

Calloway stepped into the Dregs thinking, *this is probably going to get me killed*, but he couldn't help the rush of adrenaline pumping through his veins. After the fight in the alley, he and the twins were out for retribution, and he'd be damned if anyone would stop them. It was quite apparent that he had become the secret weapon since he'd been out of town for so long. Not a single soul in here looked familiar from the old days, but he did recognize Kilian from the description he'd been given sitting in the corner with some of his followers.

Initially, he'd been trying to figure out a way to claim a spot at any table closest to his target, but Kilian and his men were being so loud and boisterous that he was able to simply grab a stool at the bar and still hear everything they were saying. The fool was drunk and boasting about how he took the Rogue down a peg tonight. *Sure you did, scum. Except that Aedrik wasn't even there. And you were fighting his sister. And you ran away. Sure you did.* The way Kilian was going on, he made it sound like he had defeated Aedrik himself tonight in that alleyway.

Calloway didn't even bother looking in their direction. He felt if he did, he would start laughing out loud, but suddenly Kilian started talking about something that was actually of interest to him.

"You should have seen the looks on their faces when they saw the Big Man's face! Ha! Weren't expecting him to be on our side," he boasted once again, making it seem like the whole idea had been his from its inception.

One of Kilian's cronies shouted out drunkenly, "Yeah! That was really cool how you got him to help us, Kilian!" Kilian just smiled at the guy, knowing the poor drunk was sucking up to the "Man-who-would-be-king," but he never actually took credit in so many words. It was clever of him to let them infer that he was smarter and more powerful than he truly was, but Calloway had his doubts about Kilian being the one to sway Deorick's loyalties. In fact, by all accounts, Deorick had been the bane of Kilian's existence until recently.

No way.

Someone else must have managed to sway him in that direction. You don't just throw away a lifetime of friendship to help a Rogue wannabe who ultimately stands no chance at the title.

Besides, this sounded like an extremely recent development. Ashdan had commented on Deorick's cagey behavior as if it was unusual. Calloway wouldn't have known to take note of it otherwise. The "Big Man" had something else going on and if Calloway had to bet, he would say that Deorick was more of a danger than a help to Kilian's pursuits.

That didn't stop Kilian from basking in the praise. He pushed his shoulders back and sat up a little taller. That was when he noticed Calloway at the bar. Calloway knew the moment the man's eyes were on him because a hush fell over the room and Kilian stood.

He plopped his lean body into the seat next to Calloway's and turned toward him, demanding his attention. Calloway looked up from the drink he'd been pretending to nurse for the last several minutes as if just noticing Kilian for the first time.

"Can I help you 'somfin?" Calloway asked, using the Southern Common accent he'd heard everywhere on the streets in the Capital. Kilian seemed to register that before he spoke. Apparently, he wasn't oblivious. "You're new around these parts." It wasn't a question, but Calloway nodded obligingly anyway. "And what brings you to the Thieves' City?" He gestured around them illustratively as if they were taking in a grand view and the men behind him let out hearty chuckles and guffaws.

Calloway knew he had to tread carefully here. "I's workin' as 'is Majesty's Hostler, but 'e didn' like the way I brushed the ol' mare. Gave me the boot, he did. Nice place to do it too, no 'fence."

Kilian chuckled at his explanation, clapping him on the back. "None taken, friend. You look like a capable enough fellow and we're always looking for new recruits. If you've no need to rush back to Tsifira, why don't you stay and train with my boys a while. I could see a man like you doing well here. Assuming you're able to follow orders. Mind you, you won't be getting anywhere near my horse, *no offence,* but we have plenty of other employments to occupy you."

Calloway could not believe his luck. He pasted a big dopey smile on his face. "Can I ever! I's no good at brushin' horses, but I can swing a blade w' the rest of 'em!"

Kilian's grin became genuine. "Then in celebration of your new employment, I insist you have another drink, on us."

He dragged Calloway with a newly filled tankard over to the table where they were sitting. The other men greeted him warily but happily enough. Calloway understood he would have to prove himself with these men. They were the bottom of society's barrel and didn't trust easily, but once he was in, he would be able ask them anything. They were cautious, but not criminal masterminds. That title was reserved for Aedrik, Aedrian, and Ashdan.

The minutes turned into hours, but Calloway didn't feel he could learn anything more tonight. The men grew more and more boisterous as they guzzled down pint after pint like it was the end of the world. Calloway managed to make it look like he was drinking as much as they were—nothing made men more suspicious than another man refusing alcohol—but quietly he employed a few handy tricks he'd learned in the Guard to make the drink disappear without imbibing.

He listened carefully as Kilian grew more and more boastful over his fight with the "half-breeds." Kilian was apparently the type to spin tall tales the more he told a story. Pretty soon, he was single-handedly defeating the Rogue and all of his men.

Calloway was incredibly thankful that Ashdan had left them with a glamour just before departing with the Prince or he would probably be dead on the floor right about now. He hadn't fought Kilian personally, but if the other man had recognized him, he would have been done for. There were several mentions of a guy with "white-blonde hair" who was working with the Rogue. This glamour darkened his hair to a dirty blonde and added a bit of weight to his face. Aedrian's had barely changed his most recognizable features which was why he'd remained outside. Ashdan had really only gifted them with enough so that if someone passed them on the dark streets, they wouldn't take a second look. Even these simple effects would be gone in a few days. They needed to work fast.

Something interesting caught Calloway's attention after a while—Kilian made no mention of the Key. Either he didn't know about it, or he had finally figured out how to keep his mouth shut about something.

Eventually, the party started breaking up and Calloway endured several drunken back pats of various intensities on his way out the door. Kilian walked beside him. He didn't see any sign of Aedrian, but hadn't expected his friend to wait around all night. Kilian placed a hand on his shoulder, halting their trek and forcing Calloway to look at him.

"Well, my new friend, I will see you tomorrow. But you should know. I have a single chance policy. Cross me and you die." He looked right in Calloway's eyes so there would be no miscommunication.

"Understood." Calloway let his eyes widen just a little so Kilian would think he had put the fear of the gods into him. Kilian clapped him on the shoulder smugly and they parted ways.

Making sure he wasn't followed; Calloway made his way to Aedrian's living quarters. Aedrian lived in a relatively nice part of the city, in an apartment that strategically looked out over much of the lower district. It was here Calloway would go into hiding while the uproar over the Prince surged and ebbed. Once they figured out the Prince was no longer in the city, their search would take them elsewhere and Calloway would be able to move a little more freely.

Elite Guardsmen were roaming the city already, arresting anyone who looked suspicious. Normally, the three of them would have done everything they could to make sure those people didn't remain wrongfully imprisoned, but until they could clear their own names, they were forced to make some sacrifices.

Calloway climbed the hidden hand holds on the outside of the building that led to the roof. He vaulted deftly over the top and looked around; it didn't look as though anyone was there, but looks could be deceiving. His suspicions were confirmed when a low voice called from the shadows, "I thought you'd never get out of there. Those barbarians were awfully glad to add to their ranks."

Calloway shrugged and moved to sit next to Aedrian. "They just want to gather anyone into the fold who has a bone to pick with your status quo. My first day on the job is tomorrow."

"I was there for that part." Aedrian let out a low chuckle that was utterly decadent, and Calloway found himself forgetting what they were talking about. All he knew was he wanted to hear that laugh again.

"Come on. Let's go inside and celebrate." He pulled Calloway to his feet and dragged him down the stairs into his home. "Now you can drink for real. And none of that swill they serve at the Dregs." He held up two glasses full of strong dark liquid. A twinkle appeared in his cobalt blue eyes. "Here's to treason, betrayal, and vengeance."

Calloway shook his head. "To us, reuniting."

Aedrian's eyes flashed, and he stepped closer, touching his glass to Calloway's. Calloway touched his glass to Aedrian's and drank deeply. It had nothing to do with the alcohol when he grew flushed and a little dizzy at the other man's nearness.

Ever the observant one, Aedrian stepped even closer until there was only a breath between the two men. His eyes burned into Cal's and said, "How else should we celebrate this reunion, then?"

Without think further, Cal grabbed Aedrian's hand and pulled him into the darkened bedchamber beyond the kitchen.

It was time for some dreams to be realized.

Chapter 11
Ashdan

Ashdan woke from her light sleep to the sound of bitter cursing. She sat bolt upright, her claws unsheathed out of habit, but it was merely the Prince attempting to escape from his bonds by chewing through the plant-ropes. She had to give him credit—short of having anything sharp, he had resorted to the next best thing.

There were green smudges on the small rocks sitting around his feet—marks of his other attempts at releasing himself. In theory, he should already be free and riding hard back toward the city. In reality, every bite mark or scrape he inflicted upon the ropes healed over within seconds and seemed to make the rope stronger than it had been before. The poor guy finally noticed her watching him.

"That's some pretty handy magic you got there," he said sarcastically.

"Thanks." She wasn't going to tell him that it wasn't her spell. She couldn't manipulate plants worth a damn, but the less he knew about her and her weaknesses, the better. He seemed to accept this when she didn't say anything more, as if he'd been expecting her answer.

His face settled into what she had begun to think was now its permanent expression—a steady glare that she was sure could burn holes through lesser men and women. She simply gave him an enigmatic smile, wondering what it would be like nibble on those perfect lips. *Whoops. Down girl.*

She held in the laughter that threatened to bubble up as his lips twisted in frustration. The corner of her disguise's eyes crinkled, making her look gentle and matronly. This young man might not be the dunderhead prince she'd thought he'd be, but he would have to try a lot harder to get past her.

She made a show of curling back up on her sleeping pallet. "Go back to sleep. We ride at first light."

Ashdan could tell this was not a man used to being ignored, so when she turned around to face away from him and rolled herself back up into her blanket, she had to stifle another chuckle. "I hope you like sleeping on the ground, Your Highness, because that's going to be our bed for the next two weeks at least." She heard an exasperated groan behind her before everything fell blissfully silent again.

This was good. The more she could keep him uncomfortable and on his toes, the easier it would be to control him.

Chapter 12

Emyr

They had been riding for a few hours already, having gotten up with the dawn, when Emyr spotted something in the distance—possibly a fellow traveler. If that was the case, he thought maybe he could call out to them for help...Or maybe they would kill him for being the Crown Prince...Or they were in league with the woman and were coming to join her on the journey to wherever she was taking him.

He decided he would wait until they got closer, then decide. In the meantime, he didn't mention anything to his captor. If she was taken by surprise, he might be able to escape.

She seemed content to ride beside him in silence. She had spoken little this morning except to tell him they were nearing the edge of the desert and would have fresh water soon. Whatever was going on in that crafty little head of hers was not likely to be shared with him any time soon.

When he had asked about bathing to get rid of some of the dust she had cut him off tersely with the excuse of not having time to cater to his spoiled tendencies. Clearly, she was hiding something, but it had so far proven impossible to pry anything out of her. She was disconcertingly self-contained and Emyr had to admit he'd met his match when it came to considering all possible outcomes to a situation.

The horses suddenly sped up when she called to them in the language of the Mountain People. He finally had an answer as to whether she had Elymas blood or not. Only Elymas tribes spoke that language. But small victory of information aside, he realized she had urged the horses on because the traveler in the distance was getting closer. So much for catching her off guard. "I'm not surprised you didn't say anything earlier. I wouldn't have in your position, but I am surprised you spotted them at all."

Damn. She had known all along that he'd seen them.

"Are we going to try and outrun them?" He could see now that it was a group of five or six men.

"We will try. From what I can see, those men are part of a group of bandits that like to terrorize people traveling through the desert. If we give them the chance, they will kill us both. I don't plan on dying today, do you?"

Emyr took this information in for a moment, not dignifying her question with an answer.

"They might kill *you*, but surely they won't kill the Crown Prince of Jesimae. Not when I'm so much more valuable to them alive given the reward I'm sure my father has placed by now on my safe return home."

She let out a hoarse laugh and urged the horses faster. They were in a full-on gallop now and had to yell over the sound of the horses' hooves. "I'm sure they *would* keep the Crown Prince alive...if he were here."

What?

She handed him a small looking glass that he had seen many women carry on their person. It was a struggle not to drop it from the galloping horse with his tied hands, but he managed to look into it for a split second. What he saw shocked him to the core. A young ruffian stared back at him. Blonde messy hair framed a rugged face full of scars. The man looked broader than Emyr in the shoulders, but younger by a good ten years.

He threw the glass back to her and she caught it with one hand, sliding it immediately back into her pack. "I knew you were disguising *yourself*, but I didn't know..." He shook his head in disbelief.

The motion lowered his head just enough that the arrow flying past didn't kill him on the spot.

The woman turned toward their pursuers and flung a knife with deadly accuracy into the eye of the one in front. In that instant, he was glad he was with her. It was her fault they were in this situation, but he would not have been able to fight off six—no, five now—men by himself on horseback.

"EMYR!"

He yanked his gaze from the men coming at them. She was holding out his sword.

"If we get out of this alive, I'll get rid of your bindings permanently, deal?"

He nodded grimly. He was not under any illusions; the only way she would let him go free would be if she was killed in this fight. But if she was killed, then he would likely be dead too. Better to stick to the evil you knew. He grabbed the sword with his bound hands and shouted, "Deal!"

The bindings slithered off of his hands and feet and knotted themselves around the pommel of the saddle. Well, that was handy.

A few heartbeats later, the men were upon them. She threw another knife that hit its target squarely in the chest. The man fell off his horse, dead. Two down. Elated to have free use of his arms, Emyr swung his sword up and blocked the killing blow from another attacker. The man's horse veered away in terror, but he steered it back until their legs were nearly touching and attacked again.

Emyr blocked blow after blow.

The man was good, but was tiring from the heat and the suffocating leather armor he wore. He wasn't used to his prey fighting back so effectively. Emyr was in his element. He always felt most alive on the battlefield and had fought many of his father's wars since he was a teenager on this horse's back. Baela was unflappable and responded to the lightest pressure of his knees.

A few more swings and Emyr was through his guard. He swung a final time, nearly taking the man's head off. As the body slid to the dead earth below, Emyr grabbed the reins of the man's horse and used it as a buffer against the next man trying to close in. A glance told him the woman had already taken out another of their attackers, leaving two in pursuit.

The one next to the woman raised his hand and his hood fell back. The black markings covered his face and hands. He was Elymas. The other men had been normal and non-magical, but clearly this one had been holding back until the situation became dire.

Emyr would have to say that four out of six in your party dying was pretty dire. The man's eyes didn't appear angry, however. Instead, he looked positively gleeful at having found a worthy opponent.

The markings on his face began to glow an unnatural green and a ball of fire grew in the man's hand. Emyr had no shield, no way of defending himself, but when the man unleashed the ball of green flame, the woman threw up a hand and it dissipated as if it had hit a wall. She shot back with a bright blue bolt of her own, but it didn't seem to do much but turn his cheeks red from its heat.

While the two of them began to trade magical blows, the last man tried to wedge his horse between hers and Emyr's. Emyr half stood in the stirrups, turning his body, and ran the man clean through. He yanked his sword out as the body tumbled to the cracked earth below. The remaining man was furious now and seemed to decide on a change of tactic. He had stopped throwing balls of fire and let them pull ahead a few feet, but his glyphs were pulsing stronger and stronger. The woman looked alarmed as she turned to Emyr and gestured for him to push his horse faster.

She shouted a word in the same mountain dialect he'd heard earlier, and the horses were suddenly in a flat out sprint, mouths frothing from the exertion. Emyr didn't see what the purpose would be of going faster. They were in open land with nowhere to hide, but suddenly they crested a hill and he thought he would cry at the sight of the river that stretched out to either side of them. On the other side—trees. Cover. But. How to cross?

"Go! Go! Into the water! He can't follow us when he's that magically charged!" Emyr had heard the rumors that too much magic and water didn't mix well, but had never seen it confirmed. Fortunately for them, the rumors seemed to be true.

As they approached the water, the terrain changed. Small shrubs dotted the banks, and the cracked dryness gave way to softer and softer earth. The four horses plunged into the water—Emyr still held the reins to the horses of the men who had attacked them. It was cold and Emyr was immediately drenched to the waist. The horses' feet barely touched the bottom while they tried to keep their heads above water, but they were slowly making progress toward the opposite bank. It would have to be enough.

The woman was urging the horses on consistently in that strange tongue. They responded, but it took a second for them to obey. Emyr glanced back when they were about halfway across. The man rode back and forth along the bank, his horse pacing restlessly. Green fire crackled along his glyphs, pulsing and leaping off his skin. He looked like a small green sun, gleaming from the far bank. Whatever he had been planning, it seemed to avoid the water completely. He released a massive amount of raw magic in their direction, but Emyr needn't have even ducked. The second it was over the water, it fizzled out and disappeared in a rather beautiful shower of sparks.

At the same time, Emyr felt the bottom of the river begin to slop upward again. They had managed to cross safely. He was soaked to the bone, but alive. The woman spoke to the horses again and they hurried into the trees. "We're not safe yet. As soon as he is no longer charged with magic, he will cross and come after us. We need to be far from here." They kept the horses moving for at least another hour before he realized that something was different.

Emyr stared at the woman. When she had spoken, her voice had been softer, younger. Her body seemed to shift and morph in front of his eyes. When she saw his expression, she sighed. "Damn water." Before she finished speaking, her skin finished shifting and settled, but the woman he had been traveling with for the last two days was no longer there. In her place was a younger, devastatingly beautiful woman with piercing green eyes and mahogany hair.

Chapter 13
Ashdan

Ashdan couldn't figure out why he wasn't sitting there staring at her in horror, or at least trying to kill her. Either would have been preferable to his calm practicality. Her disguise was completely gone and the glyphs that marked her as something other than human stood out starkly against her damp skin.

Their impromptu swim in the river had washed away any chance she had of hiding, but he had dismounted his horse and was methodically ringing out his belongings. The glamour she had placed on him when she saw the bandits approaching washed away as well, and he was back to his stupid-handsome self again.

Finally, soaking shirt in hand, he turned to her. "Why didn't you just let them take me? Wouldn't that have made your life easier?"

She snorted. "Hardly. I have plans for you that don't involve you dying. Why aren't you running away from me in terror? Or at least to get away? Most people who see my kind don't want to get within ten feet." She tactfully failed to mention the other reason most people didn't want to be anywhere near her. Him knowing *what* she was could be only slightly better than him knowing *who* she was.

Now it was Emyr's turn to snort. "I am going to be king one day—that is, assuming you let me live." His sardonic smile faded. "If that is true, I must lead *all* of my people. Not just the ones society deems appropriate, but every. Single. One. I don't see a purpose in alienating some of the most talented, powerful, and useful members of our land just because their culture is misunderstood, or they have markings on their skin that I don't." He fell silent, contemplating an argument he'd clearly had before. "As for getting away, I think you've more than proved that's not an option. Of course, that doesn't mean I'll stop trying."

Ashdan didn't want to respect him—she had a job to do that didn't involve seeing him as a real person—but she couldn't argue that he would make a great leader one day. It did not escape her notice, however, that he was the seventh person ever to see her true face.

Three of them were family, two might as well have been, and one was dead. Now this man who she really knew nothing about other than his station in life had witnessed something she never showed anyone. Something would have to be done about that...maybe Aedrik knew a spell that would make him forget what he'd seen.

She would have to remember to ask him when she got back to the city.

Chapter 14
Calloway

Calloway watched the brutish men laugh and shove each other down the street. For days now, he'd been working his way closer to Kilian, using Aedrik's more rudimentary disguises. But he wasn't close enough yet that he didn't have to eavesdrop on conversations. That would take time they couldn't really afford, so he split his time between sucking up to the disgusting bastard and following around his closest friends.

Today they were headed down Wind Street for some reason. None of the men lived near here and there weren't any bars or brothels to frequent. Their motives soon became clear, however, when they reached the end of the street and stood waiting by the city's outer wall. There was a massive drainage tunnel here that had been rusted over for years. Convicts and fugitives sometimes used it to escape the city if they were desperate enough, but it didn't look as if it had been opened in quite some time. It was one of the more dangerous passages out of the city, given to sudden flooding at certain times of the day.

It didn't look as though these men had brought any provisions with them for a journey. That meant they had to be waiting for someone. Would they attempt to escape somewhere without Kilian? Calloway found out the answers to all his questions only when two large hands grabbed him and threw him against the opposite wall, slamming his head against the hard stone. The men by the drain turned and launched themselves at him before he could recover. "I knew he was no good." Punch.

"Not to be trusted!" Kick.

"Who you working for, Scum?" Kick, kick.

"Must be the Rogue," said a slightly smarter one. "That's how he's been closing in so easily!" Calloway struggled against his captors and managed to get several good swipes in with his small wrist dagger, but there were too many even for him. "Let me take a turn, boys." Finally, the men backed away to make room for Kilian.

Someone ripped the knife out of his hand and handed it to Kilian who bent over until his face was inches from Calloway's. The small, but wickedly sharp blade slowly and agonizingly entered the space between his ribs and the last sound he heard was Kilian's soft whisper, "If you live, send the brothers my regards. Although, I suppose this will get the message across either way." Calloway's vision flickered, blinking out the sight of another familiar face that belonged to the hands that had grabbed him initially, and he knew no more.

When he woke, the men were gone and the grate covering the Wind Street Tunnel was slightly off its hinges, irreparably damaged from their attempts to pry it loose from its rusted seat. He spent an agonizing few minutes trying to sit up and finally managed to get to his feet. The wounds themselves wouldn't kill him—his knife's blade was too short, and his ribs were merely bruised—but there was a reason no man who encountered Calloway's knife lived to tell the tale. If he didn't get a certain kind of antidote soon, he would be dead and of no use to Aedrian or his brother.

Thinking of Aedrian helped him straighten and start moving. He wouldn't let Kilian end what had only just begun. They'd waited years to be together. Calloway refused to have it all end by his own knife.

Stumbling and using the alley walls for support, Calloway slowly began the trek back to his friends. They would be able to help him—assuming he arrived before the poison took full effect. It was a small consolation that several of Kilian's party also bore similar wounds. They would be dead by the time they left the long tunnel.

He stuffed the knife back in its sheath, gritted his teeth, and kept going if for no other reason than to deliver the news he carried with him. Aedrik and Aedrian must know what had transpired here. This was the information they had been waiting on since the moment they'd seen the faces of the ones who'd ambushed them when they were escaping with the Prince.

Chapter 15
Aedrian

Since the kidnapping of the Crown Prince, the city had been placed under martial law—no one was allowed to enter or leave, and the Governor had set a strict sundown curfew. Of course, the main gate and the harbor were not the only two ways out of the Thieves' City. Especially if you knew what you were doing. Aedrian, Aedrik, and Calloway strongly suspected that Deorick had fled the city through one of these routes, but were putting off chasing after him in favor of waiting for one of Aedrik's Eyes to bring word of a sighting. Jesimae was a big country, and it would not serve them to chase after the man only to find they'd been going in the wrong direction and added weeks to their pursuit.

Besides, Calloway's "job" with Kilian was proving to be quite fruitful. They had been able to preemptively stop two of his planned riots and make their interference look like accidents. It had only been a couple of days, but he'd overheard two of Kilian's closest friends talking about plans to leave the city. It was why Aedrian had sent Cal to follow them tonight.

Aedrian hadn't been the least surprised to hear the news. Before anyone else, Kilian would save himself. Even if that meant abandoning his followers to Aedrik's vengeful wrath. So, the brothers began to gear up once again for a long journey. It wouldn't be long, Aedrian could feel that something was about to change.

In the meantime, they flitted from hideout to hideout, narrowly avoiding the Elite Guard who were still after the Prince's kidnappers. The Rogue had taken official responsibility for the kidnapping of Prince Emyr and sent a note directly to the King with their demands. So far, there had been no reply except that in the form the Guard rampaging through the city searching for them.

No matter, Aedrian knew his brother was prepared to wait for as long as it took and would take whatever measures necessary to achieve his goal. It was why they were sending Emyr to their mother's fortress in the first place. They needed a place far from Angerona that only they had access to and that the savvy Prince couldn't escape from.

It was only when Calloway stumbled into their current hideout with a busted-up face and several knife wounds that Aedrian found his confidence shaken. He knew he was about to get some answers, but first they needed to make sure that Calloway wasn't about to die.

He stood quickly, knocking over the large chair he'd been sitting in, and rushed to the side of his close friend and lover. "What happened?" he asked, catching Calloway and sitting him down before he could fall.

"Kilian. I was following the inner circle, but they'd apparently caught on to me and decided to have some fun with me before they escaped. They left me for dead and then fled down the Wind Street tunnel." He paused, giving Aedrian a meaningful look. Aedrian cursed a blue streak as he gathered healing supplies from one of his cupboards. They both knew that the Wind Street tunnel, if followed far enough, would take a person out of the city.

Aedrian felt his heart start beating in anticipation of the chase. He asked a question to confirm the obvious, "Kilian was with them?" Calloway nodded and stretched out on the long, plush sofa. He grabbed Aedrian's hand and locked eyes with Aedrik who had just entered the room.

"It was Kilian, but—the Traitor. He was with them." Aedrian's blood began to boil. So, it was official, then. Deorick was in league with Kilian.

Pondering what could have possibly possessed the man to switch sides would take too long. It was simply baffling. They needed to hunt them down and cut off this threat at the head. But first things first.

Aedrian continued rummaging in cabinets for the proper plants, ointments, and bandages. Neither brother was exceptional with healing, but between Aedrian's gift with living things, and Aedrik's gift with spells, Cal would be back to his normal self in a couple of days.

"Aedrian."

Cal's voice came roughly from the couch where Aedrik was bent over his wounds, his glyphs glowing dimly. He turned. "Kilian stabbed me with *my* knife." Both brothers cursed this time and Aedrian grabbed an extra ointment.

"Damn fool. What? Did you give him the knife and *ask* him to stab you?" Cal gave him a death glare and winced as Aedrik poked a particularly tender spot on his ribs. Then he gave a harsh chuckle.

"No, but even you couldn't have taken on Deorick plus half a dozen murderous minions. I think Kilian will find that his party will be decreasing significantly in the next few hours."

Aedrian acknowledged this fact with grim satisfaction, but decided to focus on the matter at hand.

"Get out of the way, Aed. Your magic's not fully back yet. You can't help all that much and you'll be useless if he dies of the poison from his own blade."

Aedrik gave his brother a reproachful glance, but rolled his eyes and backed away. Aedrian knew that he would be dead for speaking to the Rogue like that if he was anyone but Aedrik's twin brother. Luckily, his brother loved him and understood that Aedrian was the best person to handle this situation. Admitting each other's strengths and weaknesses was what kept them and their friends alive.

Aedrian bent over Calloway's wounds and began cleaning them. He tried to ignore the other man's hisses of pain when the ointments stung and fizzed on his body, but found it was distinctly harder to give tough love to someone you had romantic feelings for. He had to keep telling himself he was saving the man's life. It didn't help that Calloway was also distracting him by trailing his fingers over the glyphs on his bare arms.

"Stop it. I don't want to stab you with this needle."

"What's one more stab wound? You could just heal that for me too while you're at it."

Aedrik snorted at Calloway's comment.

"Guess he's feeling better already. I'm gonna go...get the horses and supplies together. Meet me downstairs in a half an hour."

Alone, the two men looked at each other and then burst out laughing. Calloway clutched his stomach and pulled himself together, wincing with pain even as he shook with mirth.

"I think we made him uncomfortable. He was out of here faster than I've ever seen him move. And that's saying something."

"Aed's happy for us. He just doesn't know how to act around us now that things are different. We've all been friends for years. I bet he never thought he would have to worry about the two of *us* together. Also, we kind of picked some pretty lousy timing."

Calloway shrugged and managed to sit up. The color had returned to his cheeks already and Aedrian had finished patching him back together. He was still weak, but he would live. They couldn't say the same for the few men who had also caught the business end of his special little knife. It was time to go after what remained of Kilian's merry band of scumbags. Aedrian pulled his friend to his feet and handed him a clean shirt.

"Meet you downstairs." A slightly manic grin crossed his face as anticipation for a fight set in. "Time to go hunting."

Chapter 16
Aedrik

Half an hour later, the three companions were skirting through the city, using every back alley and hidden passage they knew. Since all three were at the top of the King's most wanted list, it would not do for them to be caught because they failed to be cautious. They had also fully shed their faded glamours.

Soon they reached the city's edge, and the Wind Street Tunnel came into view. The grate that normally covered it was slightly askew and looked like its edges had been hacked at continuously by someone in desperate need of entrance to the tunnel. Aedrik shook his head. Stupid. Kilian was leaving a trail for the Elite Guard to follow, not to mention Aedrik and himself.

They would have to be extra careful now. If someone had seen or heard Kilian's group escaping through the tunnel, they might have thought they were helping the Rogue by sending the Elite Guard after the Rogue's enemies. They would have no way of knowing that they were also sending the Guard after the men who had been protecting them for years.

Aedrik considered it his brother's bad influence that he didn't immediately seek out any witnesses and have them killed. He saw that as necessary for the protection of their way of life, but he wouldn't have a life for very much longer if either of his siblings found out what he had done to said witnesses. So be it. Any Guards that came after them would be thrown directly in the path of his brother. He could take care of them and be happy about it.

Aedrian dismounted and pulled the heavy grate aside. Aedrik glanced at Calloway as the wounded man tried to dismount.

"You gonna be able to keep up, blondie?"

Calloway shot Aedrik an obscene gesture with his free hand.

"Guess that answers that," Aedrik said, climbing off of his own horse.

"Right," Aedrian said, wiping sweat from his brow, "it's on foot from here, boys. The tunnel is several miles long and kind of a pain to navigate, so we better get started because I want to be out of there by nightfall. One less chance of dying." He grabbed the reins of his horse and walked almost jauntily to the entrance without looking back at the other two.

Aedrik turned to Calloway. "And they say *I'm* obsessed with danger."

The other man shrugged.

"He's *your* brother. It'd be strange if you didn't have *something* in common."

Aedrik laughed, "Just as long as you don't expect *me* to kiss your boo-boos too."

Calloway flashed him another obscene gesture, but grinned back.

Aedrik gestured for Calloway to precede him. It was best if the injured man didn't bring up the rear. Besides, his brother would never forgive him if he let something happen to Calloway. Aedrik was happy for his brother, but he hoped this new development wouldn't affect his brother's work.

He would never admit it to Aedrian's face, but he would not have remained Rogue for long if it weren't for his brother's common sense and ability to govern the common people with benevolence. In another life, Aedrik was convinced Aedrian had been a ruler of some sort. And not a crooked one either. Perhaps one of the First Kings.

He slid the grate back into its rightful place then turned and led his fretting horse into the darkness and damp. "Easy now, boy. The darkness only lasts so long."

Chapter 17

Emyr

Emyr was hardly concentrating on riding because he was too busy wondering what in Aglaeca's Hell that morphing spell had done to his body. It was easy to blame the Jesiman people's god of the dead, but he felt sure it had to be some kind of reaction to the woman's magic.

His skin had been crawling in the most unsettling way since they'd left the riverbank. It was as if the lower layers were shifting beneath the top one. Another roll of his shoulders had the woman looking over at him in concern. He'd been trying to hide the reaction from her, but finally he didn't feel there was any point.

"What did you do to me? Why am I about to jump out of my skin? I thought you said the water washed away the magic. Is this some kind of residual reaction?"

He finally gave in to the urge to rub his hands up and down his arms. He turned to her angrily, ready to demand answers, but the look on her face gave him pause. She looked surprised, concerned, and...curious? "What? What is it?"

"Well, it's just that...that river. Normal water washes away most common spells, but isn't too effective. *That* river has certain...properties. I'd been trying to avoid submerging either of us because I have some permanent protective spells around myself that I've had to put back up now that we're dry."

He'd noticed when she had started the process as her appearance had begun to change again very subtly.

"It takes a lot of magic to cast those spells, but—" Here she stopped and considered her next words carefully. "That river is known for being especially powerful when it comes to erasing enchantments. Ones that would survive a submersion in any other river can't seem to stand against this one. The river's true name is Nairna, but around these parts it is known as the 'Magician's Comeuppance.'"

"What are you saying?" She gave him a look that said, "Come on. You're not stupid."

"But I don't have any particularly powerful enchantments on me. I think I would know that, right?" As he said this, his skin gave an unsettling ripple. When he looked down at his bare arms, he noticed that there was a visible change in his normally smooth, olive-toned skin.

"Gods! What is happening?" He looked desperately at his traveling companion. Somewhere in the confusion of the attack, escaping, and their talk earlier at the edge of the woods, he had stopped thinking of her as captor. A dangerous turn of thought, certainly, but right now she was the one with all the power. Not to mention, the one keeping him alive. She was also the one who had all the answers and boy, did he need some now.

As they continued to ride and he writhed in his saddle, she began to tell him the story of the Magician's Comeuppance.

"Many, many years ago, this land was not a part of Jesimae. It was free country under the domain of the different tribes that still lay claim to the North. I believe it was your grandfather who conquered this part the first time and claimed it for the 'Glorious Realm.'"

Emyr didn't miss the sarcasm in the way she referred to his family's conquests. He supposed many people still felt that way, but he couldn't stop the defensiveness from rising. He bit back a retort and let her continue.

"Anyway, this was centuries still before your grandfather was even born. At that time, this area was plagued by a dark sorcerer. People were so afraid of him that travel through these woods was almost at a complete standstill and his name was whispered in the hushed tones of one expecting any minute to be their last. His name has since been lost to history, but no one has forgotten his last stand.

The woodland people finally convinced an Elymas tribe nearby in the Licean Mountains to send a team to help. They arrived in one of the villages just as he was finishing burning it to the ground and gave chase. He attempted to fight back, but though he was strong, there were too many for him to conquer on his own.

His black forbidden magic took out two of his pursuers before he was forced to the edge of the river. As soon as the water touched his boots, his strength began to wane and when he was submerged to his waist and unable to move, the few Elymas who were still alive bound the water into his very being. They cast a spell so powerful that he was destroyed from within. Since then, the river is still imbued with the powerful properties of that spell. *No* magic has been able to withstand its waters. That spell altered the land permanently."

She paused, then continued, "If those waters did not remove whatever spell was placed upon you, it must have been a very strong one indeed. You may never find out why it was placed unless you find the one who cast it."

Emyr had been so wrapped up in her story that he had nearly forgotten about his rumbling hide, and he looked back down at his forearms and chest. He was pleasantly surprised now to realize that it was settling down. On the other hand, his upper body now had a strange mottled look as though it was halfway through one of her morphing spells.

She was looking at him strangely now, the story long forgotten, her eyes fixed on his torso. She reached into one of her packs and pulled out a clean shirt. He caught it and pulled it gratefully over his head.

"Best to just let it run its course. I have no idea what kind of spell *was* on you, but I guess you will find out soon enough what it was hiding. I'm sorry. I wish I knew more."

He found himself laughing helplessly. This situation was a completely ridiculous. This beautiful, mysterious captor of his was taking care of him and apologizing for any affect a spell she had nothing to do with had on him. As far as kidnappings went, he was sure things could be a lot worse.

She clearly had no intention of giving him any more information about herself, but she would also apparently go out of her way to make sure he was safe. It made no sense.

Whatever sorcery had been crawling across his skin for longer than he could remember would probably not last much longer. They would both find out soon enough what it was trying to conceal.

They were making good time, according to her, but when she told him how much more time they would be on the road, he nearly attempted another ill-fated escape. He let several minutes pass in sullen silence.

Apparently, it would be another two weeks before they reached the unknown destination. He sent up a quick prayer to Faer, god of journeys. The good news was the more time he spent with her, the more he could get out of her and the more likely it was that he would be able to escape when she let her guard down.

He knew she found him attractive. The way she'd gazed at his chest and arms earlier told him that plainly enough. It felt cheap, but he considered used that to his advantage.

He wasn't expecting anyone to come to his rescue. They were already too far away, and it was clear no one knew where they were headed or she would've already had to fight off his father's men. It would be up to him to get out of this situation.

Although, that suddenly didn't hold as much urgency as it had before. Traveling with this woman—uncovering her secrets and listening to her stories—was a lot more interesting than traveling with the Royal Progress and listening to Lord Nigel's simpering over the King's "great accomplishments."

Emyr was congratulating himself on his new plan and admonishing himself for his confused feelings when she grabbed his reins and halted both their horses. "What—?" She held up her hand for silence. Emyr didn't dare disobey. Her senses would have to be much better than his given her magical abilities and knowledge of their current terrain.

She withdrew deadly-looking claws from wrist sheaths, and he immediately put a hand on his sword hilt. Before he could draw it from the sheath, a voice sounded off to their left.

"I wouldn't do that if I were you."

He peered into the gloom and spotted the silhouettes of several men, some on horseback, all heavily armed. The *snick* sound to his right told him she was retracting her claws. He let go of his sword hilt.

Several tall, worn, ferocious-looking men stepped from beneath the cover of the shadows. In the dim light it was hard to make out, but it looked to Emyr as if every single inch of the men was covered in intricate designs etched in green paint. Was it in homage to the Elymas people who lived in the nearby mountains?

Their clothing was strange too. Tan and brown trousers met soft-looking leather boots that didn't make a sound on the forest floor. On their torsos, they wore a cross-hatch of different straps that he assumed held holsters for the many bows and arrows he spotted in their hands. Great. They were surrounded by forest savages.

It was too late to bolt for the river again. They were well and truly trapped this time. Looking toward the sky, Emyr sent another prayer to Faer. *This isn't what I meant when I asked for protection and fortitude earlier.* When the men started to close in, he began to think that maybe the Trickster was intercepting his prayers.

Chapter 18
Ashdan

Ashdan was starting to think there was something wrong with her senses recently. This was the third time she'd been surrounded, and her life thrust into danger in one week. It was one thing to willingly risk her life, but another thing entirely for other people to actively seek its end.

If it weren't for her loyalty to her family, she probably would've killed the Prince after their dunk in the river and run off. Unfortunately, she was cursed to actually love her brothers and believe in their causes. And, she could admit privately, she *may* not loath the Prince *quite* as much as she'd thought she would.

She just wished these sons of bitches had waited to plan an ambush until after she had enough magic back to glamour them both fully again.

Too many people in the last few days had seen her true face and while she didn't look the same as she had when they'd exited the river, there was a close enough resemblance that someone who had seen her before might make the connection.

She couldn't get rid of the Prince for what he'd seen, but she would have no problem taking these men out. Despite her murderous thoughts, she knew she couldn't take them all. There were at least fifteen and the majority of them had bows. She wouldn't be able to get a knife in one before an arrow would sprout from her chest.

Besides, she'd lost two of her best knives in the scuffle by the river. Best to keep her own council for now and see what they wanted.

One of the men stepped forward. He was lean and vicious-looking. She remembered that the Northern villages had been in open rebellion until recently. These were men who were hardened by violence and death.

Underneath the green paint that the forest people used for camouflage, Ashdan could see that his body was heavily scarred. He was clearly in charge. The others looked to him as he began to speak.

"You shouldn't be here. Outsiders are not welcome in these woods and they do not last long."

His accent was thick as he spoke in Southern Common to them, adopting the language that most people in Jesimae's cities spoke. It was clear he preferred the native language of his tribe most of the time, but there were few outside of this area who could decipher the intricate tongues spoken by the woodland tribes. Before she could stop him, Emyr responded to the man.

"I was under the impression that these were the King's woods. The only person who can determine who is or is not welcome is His Majesty, King Besian."

There was a low hiss of anger among the men surrounding them. The mean-looking one raised a scarred eyebrow.

"Is that so? Do you know the King? Did he give you permission to walk in *his* wood? You see, the King doesn't come this far north. He may think he rules this land, but we have been governing ourselves just fine for millennia. If you want to keep your head, boy, I suggest you not put your faith in the man who has been systematically imprisoning and enslaving our people for decades. And keep that tongue from wagging or I'll cut it off."

Ashdan watched Emyr's face blanch. It was clear he had known little about his father's activities this far north. She wondered how that was possible if he was supposed to be learning to be a ruler himself. It didn't matter now, anyway. The man gestured to someone in the trees and two of the men on horses rode in closer to flank them.

"You will come with us. We will take you to the *Dasan*. He will decide whether you can keep your lives."

With that, the men flanking them took hold of their reins and began to lead their horses on. Ashdan looked around. They were completely surrounded. No getting out of this one for now.

Their one salvation: they were still traveling in the direction she wanted to be heading. She thanked the moon goddess, Magena, who she could just see coming through the trees. Her light was a welcome reassurance that all was not lost. They would find a way to continue on their journey soon.

Chapter 19
Besian

King Besian had already sweated through his finery and it was only the eleventh hour of the morning. His discomfort wasn't due to any excessive heat. No. His Majesty, King Besian, Ruler of the Sovereign Kingdom of Jesimae, the Glorious Realm was having a panic attack. There was no other word for it.

It had been five days with no word of his son, his heir, his only child. Besian knew Emyr would be laughing if he could see his father right now, but he couldn't help it.

It wasn't just the fact that the Crown Prince had been kidnapped. There were things that even Emyr didn't know about himself and in the right hands, they could be revealed to catastrophic consequences. The boy needed to be found, not just for the kingdom or his father's sake, but for his own. If certain information got out, he was as good as dead.

Besian's valet knocked and softly opened the door. The young man wore an expression of deep trepidation as he entered slowly, having had more things thrown at his head in the last couple of days than the entire time since he'd entered the Royal service.

He bowed low before Besian impatiently waved him in. The boy was young, but had proved undyingly faithful and quite useful. The King was glad there was at least one person in Jesimae who would do his bidding without question—who believed in him wholly. Everyone else wanted something from him. It was as if this boy lived to serve.

"Well?"

The boy bowed again. "Your Majesty, the Guards have returned from the mines in the south and all the nearby villages. Not a single person there has seen the Prince or heard anything—"

Besian let out a howl of rage, cutting off his valet before he could finish his report. He knocked over a particularly valuable vase, but ignored the tinkling of breaking porcelain.

The boy cringed by the door as he continued as quickly as possible, "My Lord, none of the people in the villages know anything, but there is someone who does."

Besian turned to the boy, his raged stalled momentarily.

"A man, a nomadic sorcerer, one of the bandits who has been plaguing travelers across the desert, he says he has information, but will not reveal anything without a full pardon for his crimes and a substantial reward. The Lord Governor has refused him both of these things."

"Where is he?"

"The dungeons, Sir. The Governor had him arrested as soon as he approached the gates. Apparently, this man is someone who has been wanted for many different crimes for some time. He has murdered many people with his band of nomads. The Governor is refusing to let anyone see him. He thinks the man is lying about the information and trying to prey on your concern for your son."

"We shall see. I will speak with this man myself and take his measure."

Privately, Besian was not concerned in the least about being taken in by this man. The man may be a murderer and terror of the Desert, but the King considered himself to be equally, if not more, dangerous. After all, were not they the same? Were they not both men who would stop at nothing to achieve and maintain as much power as possible?

"Take me to him. It is time I took finding my son into my own hands. It seems one can never put faith in other people when something important is at stake. I will resolve this issue and we will either have an execution or be hot on Emyr's trail before the night is through."

"Very good, my Lord." The boy scurried out of the room in the King's wake and hurriedly shut the door behind them.

Chapter 20
Aedrian

Aedrian was feeling every excruciating curve of his saddle at the moment. They had gotten through the Wind Street Tunnel in what felt like record time with a few minor incidents of wrong turns and the like, but they had continued riding for hours after exiting. They flew along the cliffs on the coast until the hard land turned even harder.

The salt mines were a day's ride away and the land seemed to be covered with a fine crust of the precious mineral. Aedrik looked like he was in his element, but Aedrian thought his brother seemed a little wild at the moment. His black hair whipped around his face in the harsh wind and his eyes were burning with the fervor of the hunt as his own had earlier. Aedrian was just as eager to go after Kilian and Deorick, but his brother seemed to gain more energy the farther and longer they rode.

"We're catching up." Aedrik was squinting into the distance. He had been in an exceptional mood ever since they'd found the bodies of the men poisoned by Calloway's knife outside the exit to the tunnel. They had been left in the positions they'd died in, dried blood caking their faces from the rivulets that had run out of their eyes and noses and their faces frozen in masks of terror.

Aedrian had shuddered at the sight and kissed Calloway soundly on the mouth in full view of his brother, thanking all the gods that Cal had made it to them in time to receive the antidote.

Now, the man sat tall astride his horse. He seemed to be improving by the minute. It helped that Aedrik had been able to do a small spell to speed the healing. It wasn't much, but it was enough for the injuries Calloway had sustained. He was back in the game and Aedrian was no longer worried for his health.

"How can you tell we're catching up, Aed?" Aedrian couldn't fathom how his brother always knew when blood was about to be spilt. It was almost like he could smell it. Like some old men in the city claimed they could smell rain coming in the winter.

"I can feel it. We'll ride for a few more hours then make camp. I have a good feeling about tonight. I think it will be especially fruitful."

Aedrian saw Calloway about to protest. There was nothing and no one out here except for them. How would that be helpful? But Aedrian shook his head, warning him not to question it. Neither of them would ever understand the workings of Aedrik's twisted mind, but that was why he was so brilliant.

Their mother used to say that he was touched by Magena, goddess of the moon and luck. He had been her favorite when they were children given his ruthlessness, but that had never bothered Aedrian. Their mother could be almost as volatile as their father. He had always preferred if neither of them paid him any attention.

If Aedrik believed it would happen, it usually did, even if not necessarily in the way they would expect. Aedrian was prepared to take his brother's word for it that they would find what they were looking for. He began to prepare himself for a fight, shifting on his horse's back and trying to loosen up his stiff and tired muscles.

They kept riding for another hour or two, keeping talking to a minimum. As the sun sank, Aedrian noticed Aedrik slowing his pace and looking around expectantly.

As quietly as he could, Aedrian pulled his curved blades from their sheaths at his hips. Calloway saw him do this and drew his sword without a sound. Aedrik had foregone the sword in favor of two wicked-looking blades with intricate hilts and painfully deadly serrations—a gift from their mother after he'd become Rogue.

Aedrian sighed. The sight of those blades meant that this fight, whenever it started, would be fierce, bloody, and a very close call. His brother was out for vengeance and to make a point. Those blades meant he wanted to get up close and personal with the traitors.

They rode on, weapons at the ready, but nothing appeared out of the deepening gloom. Just when Aedrian was starting to think his brother might have actually been wrong about a coming battle for once, they heard voices over the next salt encrusted hill. All three companions stopped and dismounted their horses, crawling to the top of the hill. A word from Aedrian had the horses staying right where they were. The voices grew louder and more recognizable.

When they peered over the edge they could see Kilian, Deorick, and three other men setting up camp. Deorick sat staring into the fire, apart from the others, as if he was trying to see some kind of message in the flames. The others were laughing and making crude jokes as if they hadn't just watched their friends die bleeding from of their eyes.

From eight, they were now down to five. An easily manageable number between the three excellent fighters. Here was where Aedrian and Calloway went into soldier mode. They both looked to Aedrik, waiting for instructions, but none were needed when he pulled out an extra knife with his non-dominant hand and watched it fly straight and true into the eye of one of the men down below. Figuring that was their cue, Aedrian and Calloway rose to their feet and crested the hill with a yell, following in Aedrik's footsteps. One down, four to go.

Chapter 21
Aedrik

Aedrik knew it was probably stupid to charge into a fight like that, but he couldn't help it—everything he had ever hated and despised was at the bottom of that dune talking and laughing like they hadn't just wreaked havoc on his life and painstakingly wrought plans. It was a moment he would probably live to regret, but he'd never been good at being the cautious brother. Besides, he had no doubt that Aedrian and Calloway would be right behind him, backing him up the whole way. They may not agree with his every move, but they would never leave him to fight this battle on his own. His thoughts were confirmed when he heard his brother and friend launch themselves over the hill after him.

Aedrik watched another one of his knives sprout from between the shoulder blades of one of the men. It wasn't a fatal wound, but it would take him out of the equation. That left three—no, make that two—Calloway took out the spare lackey with a vicious slice of his sword. Only Kilian and Deorick were left, the former's hands shaking on his sword. He knew he was doomed.

Instead of standing and fighting for his life, he shoved Deorick forward into their path, leapt onto his horse, and galloped away without a second glance. Aedrik spent a split second staring after the escaping form of Kilian, but decided it would be easy enough to catch up with him after they'd dispatched the Traitor.

Deorick was frightening when he fought. His gigantic body packed immense strength as well as surprising speed. Add in the fact that he was not in his right mind and hadn't been for days now and he fought as though he was a wild animal—no conscience, no mercy, to the death. When Aedrian had fought him earlier, he had apparently been holding back. Now, he unleashed all of his fury and attacked mercilessly.

Calloway went in low for a swipe at his legs, but was kicked into the dirt as Deorick blocked a side swipe from Aedrian. Aedrik flew into the fray, not wanting to be left out of the fun. He and his brother attempted blow after blow, but nothing seemed to land. This was, after all, one of the men who had taught them how to fight. His decades spent honing his skills and his full Elymas blood meant he had an edge even over the two of them who were deadly on their weakest days.

Calloway was entangled with the man who'd received the knife in the back, fighting several feet away, no help. Deorick had most likely kicked him in one of his still healing injuries, but he grappled fiercely with the other man.

Aedrik nearly balked when the dark eyes turned fully on him. This was a man he'd grown up with, but there was no recognition of shared history in the flat black orbs staring back at him. The only expression that registered on Deorick's face was that of pure hatred. How long must he have been planning this?

Aedrik blocked several more blows and managed to skate out of the way in time to avoid one that would have taken off his head. The whistle of the large man's dagger over his head was a little too close for comfort and Aedrik started to think he would need a new strategy to defeat the man. Deorick snarled viciously when he missed and took aim again.

Aedrik managed to knock this knife out of the air at the last second. Aedrian came in low again and successfully swiped at Deorick's ribcage. The resulting roar was ear-splitting.

Deorick turned and knocked Aedrian away, hard. Aedrik watched his brother's head hit an outcropping of rock in horror. The resounding crack echoed against the surrounding dunes before finally escaping into the hot empty air.

Aedrian lay motionless where he had landed.

Deorick's chest was heaving and there was sweat dripping from the top of his bald head down into his blood-stained clothing. It was sticking to his body and the black glyphs covering his exposed skin began to flicker a plum-red. That wasn't good. It meant he'd been dabbling in dark magic.

Given the man's hatred and now the corruption of his magic, Aedrik knew he wouldn't win in a fair fight. Gathering up what little magic he had after healing Calloway on near empty, he adjusted his death grip on his blades—no need to make the novice mistake of holding the blades too tightly.

He spun the right one in his grip as he and Deorick circled one another. Aedrik was careful to not let his magic show in his glyphs as he imbued as much as possible into his speed and strength. It wasn't much, but it might just be enough to help him defeat one of his greatest opponents to date.

Just then, he saw Calloway begin to rise from the desert floor. He had dispatched the other man. Once he was sure that Deorick's back was to the other man, Aedrik launched himself through the air at him. Surprise flickered, there and gone, in Deorick's eyes at the strength of Aedrik's attack, but he recovered quickly and managed to fend him off. The flickers of tainted light flickered out as Deorick concentrated on not getting his throat slit.

He made the briefest eye contact with Calloway who seemed to already have grasped the plan of distraction. He pulled himself fully to his feet as Aedrik and Deorick darted back and forth, trading bruising blows.

When Aedrik saw Calloway was in position, he allowed something to happen that he had been taught never to permit with a larger opponent—their blades locked and Deorick bore down on him, using his superior height and weight to bend Aedrik backwards.

The extra strength provided by Aedrik's magic only went so far. He grunted with the strain of staying on his feet. When a sinister smile of triumph spread across Deorick's face, it was all Aedrik could to stop himself from breaking loose and punching the man in the face.

He held himself in check and gave another inch. Aedrik's entire field of vision was covered by the monstrous figure in front of and around him, so he was forced to rely on his hearing for Calloway's approach. Unfortunately, the man was a ghost when it came to movement. Aedrik never heard him coming, but...

...Neither did Deorick.

The blade came out of nowhere, breaking through the leather armor covering Deorick's chest. There was no roar this time. The big man growled in pain and broke free of Aedrik to turn on Calloway. Aedrik took the opportunity to slice at the backs of his knees. Deorick fell to the ground, hamstrung.

Aedrik took his time walking around to face Deorick. Calloway finished disarming him then moved to tend to Aedrian who was thankfully just waking up. Looking down into the eyes of the man before him, Aedrik made the sad realization that the person he'd called friend and protector for so many years was gone. Ignoring his gasping as he died slowly, Aedrik leaned close and gripped his chin harshly.

"I'd like an explanation, *friend*. You owe me at least that."

Deorick spat in his face. "I don't owe you anything, brat. My loyalties are exactly where they should be."

"And where is that?"

Silence. A cry behind them sounded. Calloway had pulled the knife out of the man he'd apparently left alive and was tying him up. Aedrik turned back to Deorick, disinterested.

"Let's try this, again. After years by our sides, what made you choose to betray us now? I know you weren't serving Kilian. That's so far beneath you, it's laughable."

The smirk on his face, even as he began to cough up blood told Aedrik that he had guessed right. Kilian was a pawn in this whole scheme. He certainly hadn't gained the kind of following he had on his own. Someone else was behind this and that was who Deorick served.

"Is it the other one? The Daeva? 'Evil Spirit,' my ass. Don't tell me you've fallen prey to those superstitions."

More silence.

Aedrik knew they would not get anything more out of him. This man could withstand just about any type of torture they decided to inflict upon him, having been enslaved in the Marble Mines of the East before their mother had rescued him. Besides, he wasn't long for this world anyway.

The color had completely drained from his face due to blood loss and he was having trouble even staying on his knees. He collapsed into the sand, gasping. Aedrik watched, unmoved.

When the death rattle began in his chest, Deorick began laughing.

"The one whom I serve—" he paused to cough. "You have taken something that they wished to possess. You will see before the end, *friend*. They are everywhere. You cannot kill this enemy with your knives. And you will die knowing your whole world has been destroyed."

His chest rattled a few more times before falling still. Aedrik took in his last breath, absorbing the raw magic that was released as Deorick's life faded away. The glassy black eyes remained open and staring at Aedrik who was no longer paying attention to the dead man, but pondering his last words, trying to find some clue within them. Aedrian and Calloway walked over, their faces grave.

"You okay?" Aedrik asked his brother who shrugged noncommittally. "Well." Aedrik placed his hand gently on the back of Aedrian's head and used some of his newly replenished magic to heal the worst of the head injury he'd sustained. Stepping away, he took his brother's sword and sliced through Deorick's neck, separating his head from his body.

Decapitation wasn't standard practice, but Aedrik felt that given Deorick's final words, they couldn't take the chance of someone reanimating the body of the deadliest fighter they'd ever known. Given how dark *Deorick's* magic had become, Aedrik shuddered at the thought of his master.

Searching Deorick's clothes, they found the Skeleton Key. Aedrik slid the thong over his head, letting the powerful object resonate against his chest where it belonged. The magic within hummed contentedly, as if it recognized that it had been returned to its maker.

Over the next several minutes, they gave the same treatment to the other bodies. They put all the bodies in one pile and the heads in another, then set both piles on fire and began cooking dinner over the flames of the smaller one.

They were all silent and contemplative after the battle. One traitor had been caught and neutralized. They would catch up with Kilian soon enough.

Without his band of cutthroats, Kilian would have a hard time intimidating anyone into protecting him from the Rogue's wrath. In the meantime, they had one of his followers trussed up next to the horses. They would get what information they could and dispose of him as well.

Chapter 22
The Daeva

Deorick's master felt his life force leave him even from hundreds of miles away. Hands tipped with long, thin fingers curled into fists of rage. The plant sitting in a pot nearby burst into flames as the glyphs covering the Daeva's arms glowed with unchecked power. The timid servant standing in the corner of the room hurriedly put out the fire, then tried to sink into the stone behind him' to prevent himself from becoming a target of the Daeva's wrath.

The imposing figure stood from the cold stone throne upon which they'd been perched, making their way onto the terrace that looked southwest. Somewhere there, hundreds of miles distant, that sniveling brat had managed to kill the Daeva's most formidable asset.

It was a heavy blow, losing such a loyal servant, but no matter, there were other ways to foil Aedrik's plans and they were already in play. Soon enough the Daeva would have something Aedrik valued immensely. Then, Aedrik would make a fair trade or lose everything.

The Daeva was still ruminating on whether to kill Aedrik anyway after the trade had been made when there was a soft cough from within the room. The Daeva turned, raising an eyebrow at the servant cowering at the door.

"I've brought the materials you requested, my—uh—Daeva." Terrified, the man fell silent. He was too new and the Daeva's attempt at a reassuring smile was anything but. The thin lips might know which direction to point, but the dark eyes held no reassurance or light.

Years of abusing the dark arts in service of their ambition had stripped what little goodness there was. The people called the Rogue of the East the Daeva, a word meaning "Evil Spirit." They weren't too far off. Humanity clung to this creature like the tattered entrails used to divine the future by other black sorcerers. The anger that swept around the room disturbed the very air with its raw unchecked power.

Stories coming from the west told of a just man who ruled Angerona's criminal underworld with a velvet-covered iron hand. A man who took care of the people with the help of his twin brother and fearsome enforcers, Deorick and the Red Lady.

The people in the west were due for a rude awakening when their Rogue was dispatched.

Chapter 23
Ashdan

The Silvijan guards had led them through the forest in record time, commandeering their stolen extra horses and almost all their weapons, but Ashdan was unconcerned as of yet. They were making better time than she'd hoped. As long as they were still headed in the right direction, she felt they were actually safer with these men than without.

The forest was unpredictable at best, and having natives to guide them through would make their trek that much easier. When they needed to get away, she would find a way. Until then, she told Emyr, they would remain with the forest people.

It had given her great satisfaction when the men had been unable to figure out how to disarm her of her claws and their accompanying sheaths full of extra blades. In the end, they'd tied her hands and covered them in empty water skins, hoping the thick leather would prevent her from escaping her bonds.

If it made them feel better, Ashdan would leave her hands where they were, for now.

Emyr seemed to be coping reasonably well with his second capture that week. He'd been stripped quickly of any and all weapons and sat dejectedly astride his horse. They hadn't bothered to tie him up, assuming they'd be able to subdue him quite easily if he tried anything.

Ashdan had sent him a warning glare to just go with it. She had a feeling they were all underestimating the Prince. So far, he'd followed instructions and not tried anything. Ashdan thanked the gods that the Crown Prince was smarter than the people had given most Royals credit for.

They might get out of here alive and unidentified. So far, no one had figured out Emyr's lineage and Ashdan intended to keep it that way. There was no way of knowing whether these people were loyal to Aedrik or not, given that they lived on the border between the eastern and western halves of the country.

The man who'd spoken to them earlier rode in the front of their party, his bow at the ready. As the sun's last light disappeared from between the leaves, he held up a hand to slow everyone down.

"We cannot travel much farther without the light. We are still far enough away, right?"

He turned to the man who appeared to be his second in command.

"I cannot say. You know the stories. Even at this distance, we are still too close for my liking, but moving onward would bring us closer in the dark before it would bring us farther away."

The one in charge nodded in agreement.

"We camp here, then."

Well, if that didn't sound ominous.

The men on horses immediately began dismounting and the others helped unload supplies. Within moments, a camp had taken shape on the forest floor and a fire had been started. Pretty soon the smells of cooking meat wafted to Ashdan's nose, and she realized how hungry she was.

Gods, she hoped they offered her a little. If not, she would take matters into her own hands, but she'd rather not kill anyone until absolutely necessary. She didn't deem food to be a good enough reason for murder.

Yet.

The men pulled their prisoners down from their horses and stashed them in a far corner of the camp. This time they tied both her and Emyr to a tree at the edge of the clearing. Emyr's arms were pinned to his sides with a rope, but Ashdan had managed to unsheathe her claws within the water skins.

Should they need to, they would be able to escape. For the time being, Ashdan and Emyr were left alone. In fact, the men seemed to specifically avoid that side of the camp.

The tree they were tied to was on the far side, closest to the direction they'd been traveling. Something in this part of the woods had them all terrified. The fire had been built on the opposite side, far from the prisoners. Neither of them could feel even a breath of heat from the flames and as the darkness settled in deeper and the temperature fell, Ashdan knew it would be a long night.

The horses tied up nearby were restless, stamping their hooves and rolling their eyes. Nothing good ever came of scared horses. Ashdan began to slip out of the knots around her wrists.

"My Prince, I think we will be leaving this place tonight. Whatever's out there that's scaring them so bad, I don't feel like becoming its first victim of the night."

Emyr didn't have a chance to respond. Just then, one of the men came over with two bowls of stew.

He untied the ropes holding them to the tree to allow them to eat, but held his sword unsheathed as they shoveled the warm broth and bits of leftover meat and vegetables into their mouths. As soon as they'd finished, the ropes were tightened once again and the man scurried away, eyeing the forest behind them.

She and Emyr exchanged a glance, but before either of them could say anything, someone else stomped over, heavily armed.

It was the one who had spoken to them earlier. He glared down at them.

"Tonight will be long and cold." At this, he tossed a blanket over both of them. "Do not try to escape. You will not survive this close to the Ruins."

"The Ruins?" Emyr asked. This earned another glare, but an explanation, nonetheless.

"The Ruins are what remains of the ancient woodland people's village that was destroyed by the Dark Sorcerer."

"You mean the one that was ripped apart by the water?"

That elicited a surprised chuckle from the stern man. "Yes. That's the one. We don't know exactly what happened, but there is still powerful black magic imbued in the very timbers that the village is made of. It has…changed…the forest around it. Any who wander too close at night have never returned. It's not worth your lives or mine, for that matter, to attempt an escape so close to the Ruins. Behave for the duration of our journey and I shall see what I can do about allowing you to keep breathing." He turned on his heel and stalked away.

"Such a kind fellow. All heart." Ashdan spat. Emyr laughed.

"I'd say that's a pretty fair deal, all things considered. Question is, will we be following his orders?"

Ashdan hated the trust in his eyes. Clearly, he was willing to follow her for now as long as she remained the lesser of two evils, but it made her feel guilty. She'd drugged him, kidnapped him, forced some powerful enchantment he'd had on his body for longer than he could remember to unwind, and now their lives were in danger from both the forest people and some unknown entity that was scaring the crap out of these hard men.

She couldn't understand his accepting attitude. If their situation had been reversed, she would blame him for everything and escape the first chance she got.

Unless—he was trying to find out more information before escaping so he could go back to his father and have her and her coconspirators executed.

That must be it.

Emyr wasn't stupid or trusting. He knew better. She would have to be careful not to underestimate him. It would be all too easy to believe that the handsome, smiling face next to her was on her side when in fact, she'd never been more alone.

Chapter 24

Emyr

Emyr attempted to loosen the bonds that held him to the tree so tightly. A small piece of bark between his shoulder blades was kindly reminding him of his predicament every time he twitched.

It had been hours since they'd been given the watery stew and his stomach was clawing at his insides. The fire on the far side of camp had withered down to its embers—not that he and the woman had benefitted from it even while it burned its brightest.

Most of the camp was asleep except for the sentries he could hear passing by their tree now and again. The horses were still restless, but some had managed to calm down enough to fall asleep. The woman next to him seemed to be asleep as well, but he wouldn't bet his life on it. She had more tricks up her sleeve than anyone he'd ever met.

It was deathly cold now, which didn't make sense at this time of year, even this far north. As he watched his breath steam in front of him, Emyr listened to the nighttime sounds of the forest. At least, he tried to.

There was nothing.

Not even the insects were making noise. No wind rustling in the trees or small creatures scurrying around in the underbrush. It was getting colder, and the night's stillness was anything but reassuring. Time to wake up the one who always seemed to have a solution.

Using his foot, Emyr nudged the woman. Her eyes opened instantly, fully awake. So, she hadn't been asleep. Just like he'd thought. When he looked down, he saw that her hands were free of both water skins and rope, claws unsheathed. When he would have said something, she held up a finger and shook her head.

She was right.

Somehow, Emyr felt that his voice would release whatever was out there from the quiet stasis it was in right now. She did, however, reach up and slice silently through the bottom coil of rope.

Coil by coil, she released them from the tree. Once free, they got quietly to their feet and made their way over to their horses and saddle bags, rearming themselves with their weapons that had been stashed there. He couldn't help but be grateful that their captors hadn't been more careful and kept the weapons with them in their tents.

Then…they waited, not moving a muscle.

Pretty soon, the temperature felt like it was beginning to rise, even marginally. The sting of unnatural cold had almost given way to a more manageable freezing when a voice sounded from the tree where they'd been tied up—the sentry had noticed their absence.

Instantly, the camp was plunged back into the otherworldly cold. The man never uttered another word. The only sound was his scream of terror and agony as something pulled him into the trees. Seconds later, it was abruptly cut off and silence once again reigned. But the damage had been done.

The men began waking up, their voices uttering questions of alarm to one another. Emyr and the woman stood with their backs to the rest of the camp, facing the direction in which the sentry had disappeared and backing away from the edge of the clearing. Their weapons were at the ready. The men's voices rose as they stumbled from their tents and took stock of the situation. Seeing the prisoners escaped, they quickly surrounded them as they had in the woods, their weapons pointing at the least dangerous things in the forest.

Their talkative friend approached them.

"Where is Frederick? What have you done with him?"

Taking his cue from the woman, Emyr remained silent and kept his attention on the darkness beyond the camp. There was still no sound, but the air seemed to pulse painfully with the cold. He flexed his fingers on the hilt of his drawn sword to keep the blood moving. His body was instinctively preparing for a fight.

But to fight what?

Something was coming and Emyr had a nasty feeling that they were surrounded by something far more dangerous than Silvijan Guards. The leader finally picked up on the fact that they weren't even paying attention to the men surrounding them.

He growled something to the men in their native language who suddenly looked terrified and turned to face the woods. He turned to Emyr and the woman and said two words that, despite the cold, were the thing that finally managed to freeze Emyr's blood completely:

"They come."

Emyr wanted to ask, "Who's they?" but had a feeling he wouldn't get an answer. Out of the dead silence, a sound came through the trees. It was a rustling, like an animal, but—wrong. He turned to the woman, a question in his eyes.

She shut hers briefly before muttering in a voice that didn't travel any farther than it needed to, "I had a feeling this could be a possibility, there are legends, but I never thought—I shouldn't be surprised it's real given everything I've seen. If the legend is true, then these things move faster than you'll think is possible. Don't let down your guard for a second. And one other thing."

"Yes?"

"Cut their heads clean off or they can come back."

Emyr gulped. The men closest to them had been listening to her hushed monologue and were nodding in agreement. They knew the legends as well.

The rustling was getting closer. Hearing it more clearly now, Emyr realized just how fast these things were really moving. Suddenly, the movement stopped, and it was as if the entire world had been muted. The breath of his travelling companion next to him was the only sound.

Then, as if they were a hellish rain sent by Aglaeca himself, creatures from Emyr's own nightmares dropped from the treetops above and the Crown Prince began to fight for his life.

Chapter 25
Ashdan

They came from above. Ashdan had only half been expecting it and barely managed to get her weapon up in time to block the first savage attack.

Other men weren't so lucky, but Emyr had apparently been looking upward and praying to the gods just before because two of them were already beheaded at his feet. She stopped worrying about him and slashed with her dagger, missing but driving the thing that attacked her farther away.

It turned and jumped on one of the men. Several men were already dead, but their leader was gloriously savage as he took out—what were they? A pile of the creatures already lay beheaded at his feet.

Ashdan took out two more, sustaining several nasty cuts and gouges in the process of dodging wicked claws and dangerous fangs. These things were stronger and faster than any human or Elymas she'd ever fought. Their arms were unnaturally long and tipped with those vicious claws.

Unfortunately, Ashdan's own claws were too risky a weapon to use in this situation as they would force her to get in extremely close, so she was making due with two of her longer daggers.

She didn't fight with a sword unless she had no other option because they were big and hard to maneuver in tight spaces. The blades she now held happened to be her sharpest which was coming in handy.

Their attackers had leathery skin blackened and shriveled by the centuries, making it that much harder to cut through their stubborn necks.

Ashdan crossed her blades at the neck of the next one and wrenched her arms wide, taking off the head, but the sharp claws of another dug into her shoulders from behind. She let herself fall backwards in an attempt to crush the thing's thin frame, but it wrapped its legs around her waist and rolled until it was on top, using its wiry strength to push her into the dirt.

She shoved her dagger backward over her shoulder. The thing screamed and jerked above her and her knife left her hand, still stuck in its shoulder.

Desperately, Ashdan held its head at bay by lashing out with her elbows. Strong jaws were inches away from taking a bite out of her face. She wriggled until she was facing the monster on top of her and plunged her other knife into its side. It let out another shriek, but clawed her left arm which had been reaching for the blade still stuck inside it.

The thing's head reared back in triumph, amber lights glowing from sockets where eyes should be. Ashdan felt as if she was looking into the fiery pits of the underworld and waited for the final blow, having seemingly run out of options.

It never came.

As the monster began to lower its arm, a bright blade stained with black blood reached through and sliced off the thing's head. Emyr shoved the thing off her and pulled her blades from its dead body, handing them to her. She nodded her head in thanks, but there wasn't time for anything else. They were assaulted once more and separated as they fought for their lives, but pretty soon, the onslaught seemed to thin.

When Ashdan looked around in relief, however, she found that only five of the Silvijan Guards were still standing, including their leader. One of the monsters took him down with a harsh blow, laying open searing wounds across his green-painted face. He scrambled for his weapon, but he would never make it in time. Ashdan rushed over and beheaded the thing.

"Stay down! We'll take out the rest of them!"

She didn't expect him to listen, and so wasn't surprised when he retrieved his weapon and began to cut down the last of the beasts. She and Emyr took out several more before they were finally left alone in the middle of the destroyed camp.

The forest floor was littered with bodies, monster and man alike. The leader and two of his men remained. He turned to her, pain radiating from his eyes as his skin pulled when he spoke.

"I believe you have proven yourself enough for tonight. Both of you. We will clean up here and then you will return with us to Silvija as my guests and guests of His Majesty, King Aedrik."

Ashdan was relieved to hear that these people served her brother. She nodded to him, confirming that they too served the Rogue of the West. There had been enough loss of life. Neither of them wanted to create another enemy tonight. When Emyr stiffened at the mention of "King" Aedrik, she sent him a quelling look until he subsided and began to help with the cleanup.

They set about piling all of the bodies of the monsters together, leaving their heads in a separate pile. When they got to the men, they hesitated. "Are any of them bitten?" Ashdan asked. One of the men answered, "It's hard to tell. They're so—" He cut off, unable to continue.

"Then we know what we must do." The others nodded. They set about beheading the human corpses, not wanting the infection from the monsters to spread to their friends' corpses. A few of the bodies they touched were already that same unnatural cold that the air had been when the monsters were still alive.

These were laid somberly in the monsters' pile as it was evident they'd been infected. In the end, they had four piles consisting of bodies and heads. The uninfected men and their heads had blessing oil poured over their fires. The flames turned blue and one of the men exclaimed that he could see their friends' souls being released.

The other piles had some very different foul-smelling ointments poured over them by the leader of the men. Ashdan also cast the necessary protections over the bodies, ensuring that nothing could ever reanimate the cursed beings. These flames turned a sickly green and burned hotter than any fire made by man.

By the time they were done, light was beginning to peek through the very top canopy of leaves. They went to the horses. Many had been casualties of the fighting. Still others had broken their tethers and run for their lives.

Their luck held though because five horses, including the two with Ashdan and Emyr's saddlebags, stood cowering against a copse of trees not far from the camp. By the time they managed to calm them all down and salvage supplies from the camp and dead horses, the sunlight streamed through the trees.

Ashdan mounted in front of Emyr and two badly injured men shared a horse. Here strength was flagging. They all needed to tend to their wounds, but no one wanted to stay in this clearing a moment longer.

The others mounted individually and they all continued in the direction they'd been heading the day before. Before long, they reached an overgrown village. The small huts were old fashioned mud and sticks.

The windows were blocked by thick growth of leaves and vines. Trees grew out of some of the roofs. The chill in the air told them this was the source of the creatures from last night.

They rode through without stopping, thanking the gods they were alive and that it was daylight. Chances were, there were more where those had come from.

When they were far enough away that the chill was gone from the air, Emyr asked the question that Ashdan had seen bouncing around in his head for some time now.

"Was that—was that the village from the tale?"

"Yes." The leader's rough voice was weak with pain. They needed to get him to his village healers soon. It was not within Ashdan's power to heal wounds. Especially not while wounded herself.

"So, the creatures that attacked us last night..."

"They were the villagers. Or...what was left of them." He paused and the horror of that statement settled deep into Ashdan's bones.

"The Elymas who destroyed the sorcerer were too late to save the village. The few who managed to escape from there alive are our ancestors. They founded Silvija and never went back home. We have always hoped that one day, maybe—but it is clear that the land is cursed. Any attempt to inhabit it would spell disaster for us."

The somber statement was a death knoll to the conversation. They rode on in silence and didn't speak for many more miles.

Chapter 26
Aedrian

Kilian had gone farther than they anticipated. By the time they passed through the small village surrounding the Salt Mines, he had been gone for at least a day. They spent the night in the single squalid in, drinking watered down ale and trying to decide how to proceed.

Yesterday, the innkeeper had informed them that he'd been robbed blind the day before they arrived by a man who had taken off in the middle of the night with several of his things, but the old man couldn't tell them where or which direction he'd gone in.

Just when they were starting to despair of ever finding his whereabouts, a stroke of luck came their way late the second night, spurring the chase back to life in spectacular fashion.

Aedrian was checking on the horses in the stables when he overheard two of the stable hands speaking in hushed voices.

"That dung-eating thief stole my saddle, bags, and water skin! Help out a guy in need and this is how I'm repaid."

"I told you he looked dodgy."

"The guy was terrified and filthy. What was I s'posed to do? Turn him away? Just trying to do a good thing. He said his entire party had been killed by the desert bandits. I mean, you saw the blood all over him too."

"Those scum have *never* left survivors. You should know that by now. How many reports have we gotten of entire families that were found left out there for the birds and mice? Stay here a few years and those stars'll be wiped clean out of your eyes. I bet we'd be rewarded if we told the Rogue about him. In fact, I bet he'd give us double if we told him he moved on to Ryton to catch a ship. Bloody fool couldn't keep his mouth shut."

Aedrian found the irony of that statement as amusing as it was helpful. They would be gone before the talkative man could find them to blab again.

So, they would go South. He slid silently out of the stables and crept to the main building. Aedrik and Calloway were lounging in a far corner of the dining room, holding court. Word of the Rogue's presence had spread and people from the village had been coming to visit and pay their respects for the last two days. Normally, at so critical a time they would not have allowed the distraction, but it provided an excellent opportunity to fish for information.

He signaled to the other two and slowly, they began to extricate themselves from the crowd. He didn't dare come any further into the room or they would never get out. People respected and were loyal to Aedrik, but they loved Aedrian for his generosity and fair judgement.

They knew it was he who provided for the common law-abiding citizens of the West. Eventually, they reached the edge of the room. Aedrik turned and waved at his subjects, thanking them for coming to see him and their continued loyalty. They gazed at him in rapt attention until he was gone from the room. When they were finally through the door, all three breathed a little easier.

Aedrik chuckled. "That should have been you in there, brother. *You're* the one they love. They only pay me any mind because they're afraid I'll have them killed if they cross me. Granted, that's true, but still. I feel like you're more suited to receiving adoration and groveling than I am."

"You couldn't have gotten me to switch places with you if you'd held a knife to my throat."

Calloway coughed through a laugh. Aedrian was actually surprised at how well *he'd* handled the attention. For someone who rarely left the shadows, Calloway had taken to his position by Aedrik's side rather well.

Now they entered their room and quickly packed everything. Within minutes they were out the door. Aedrian left the innkeeper a generous payment for his services though the man hadn't wanted to charge them at all.

There was no time to lose. The longer they waited to catch Kilian, the greater the chance he would already be on a ship. His head start had grown by another day. Hopefully, he was sleeping peacefully right now, imagining he was safe and letting down his guard. Aedrian would have dearly loved to see the look on his face as they surprised him.

The trouble was, if Kilian had managed to board a ship, it would be nearly impossible to catch him until the ship arrived at its destination. Ryton ships were famous for one important reason. Their exquisite craftsmanship aside, the town boasted a particular set of ships which were imbued with a powerful magic that allowed them to sail through the rough coastal waters faster than humanly possible.

Before the sun came up that day, all traces of the three companions at the inn had been erased and they were once again galloping over the harsh terrain to find the man who was the impetus for all their problems.

Chapter 27

Aedrik

"It'll cost ya. Runnin' ships like this is expensive work. I expect you understand, yer Majesty." The man's missing teeth gave him a feral, crooked look and Aedrik suspected he'd had his fair share of less than legal business dealings back in his day.

Aedrik felt his brother's hand on his arm, stopping him from cutting the ship's captain down with a well-placed slice of one of his daggers. He was the King of Thieves. Shouldn't that be enough to get him on the ship this close to his center of power?

They had reached the city after three days hard riding and wanted to do nothing but sleep. This man's belligerence was getting on their last nerves, but Aedrik had to respect the ancient sea-weathered husk of a man. They hadn't bothered to hide their identities—not that they weren't utterly recognizable by face alone on this side of the country—and the captain was taking advantage of the fact that they could afford his services and then some.

As things stood, he had already been more than helpful, proving his loyalty to the Rogue by informing them of Kilian's latest attempt at fleeing. Apparently, Kilian had tried to haggle with the captain as well since his was the only Wind Ship currently at port. When the captain hadn't budged, Kilian had threatened him with the sword.

Big mistake, apparently.

This man was deadlier than he had a right to be at his age and had whipped Kilian's ass right off the docks. Apparently, Kilian had later found a non-magical ship to transport him to the capital, Tsifira.

This was two days ago.

If they left on the Wind Ship today, they would overtake him and get to the city in plenty of time to set up a trap and meet him at the docks. They just had to convince this hard sell of a man to take them with him.

Reluctantly, Aedrik agreed to the captain's terms. After handing him a substantial amount of gold, they boarded the ship that evening with their fresh supplies, staring dubiously at the straps that were to hold them in place for the duration of the trip.

The ship moved so fast that they would be hurled against the walls of the cabin with vicious force when it reached the destination if they weren't strapped in. The horses were spelled asleep down below by the gruff-looking Elymas woman who powered the ship.

They were offered the same treatment as soon as they entered their cabin. Calloway and Aedrian accepted, but Aedrik was curious and claimed the bunk closest to the window, pulling the straps tight around his legs and shoulders.

There was shouting above deck as the ship pulled slowly out of the harbor. He could feel the ship turn and angle itself parallel to the coast. A great bellow of "SAILORS TO BRACES!" rattled the wooden boards beside Aedrik's head. He winced. *Here we go.* An echoing bellow of, "ALL CLEAR!" rang out and they were off.

The ship gained speed at a terrifying pace. Looking out the window, Aedrik could see the vast expanse of the Great Western Sea rushing by. He squinted at the horizon, but there was no land in sight. The sea had been crossed supposedly by his mother's ancestors to build Angerona, the Black

City, but no one had ever returned who tried to find the first homeland of the Elymas.

The Great Western Sea was named as such because of its seemingly unending expanse. Everyone knew that, even though the earth was round, if you sailed west from Jesimae, you would not end up at the Eastern Continents.

You would disappear.

Pretty soon, Aedrik started to get a little dizzy and had to close his eyes. The rushing water was hypnotic, but slightly sickening. He looked over at Aedrian by the door and Calloway perpendicular to his head. They were fast asleep. Not bothered or delighted by this shocking journey—simply unaware of the ship's movement.

For a second, Aedrik wondered if he should have accepted the magical sedative, but he rather liked the new experience despite the slight discomforts. He lived for that rush that came with taking risks and this one was novel, to boot.

He closed his eyes for a while, but after about an hour, he felt the ship slow marginally.

"TURN OF THE COAST!"

The words were almost lost over the roar of the water, and Aedrik was amazed all over again. How the Captain managed to make himself heard over the crashing of the waves, Aedrik had no clue. To him, there was no other sound, but that of the water rushing past his head at breakneck speeds.

The trip to the Turn of the Coast would take at least a day aboard a traditional ship. They had reached it in an hour. Aedrik's body listed slightly to one side as the ship sped around the turn. At the rate they were going, they would be in the capital in two hours.

As the ship righted itself once again, Aedrik looked out the window. This time, he thought he could spot the islands that lay south of Jesimae far in the distance. He hadn't realized they were so close, having never left the country.

He remembered stories he'd heard from sailors as a child of the soft white sand and warmth all year round. It made him want to ask the captain if they couldn't just take a short detour…

He drifted to sleep amid thoughts of sunny islands, beautiful women, and a much-deserved break from ruling a criminal empire.

When he awoke—

"APPROACHING DESTINATION!"—he stumbled on unsteady feet up to the deck as the ship slowed to a slightly less obscene pace, he was greeted with a much grander sight.

The capital of Jesimae, Tsifira, lay resplendent in front of him and the Royal Palace glinted white and gold in the sunlight from the top of a hill. "Jewel," the name meant, and it was apt.

Colorful buildings and ships sparkled against the sun's rays, making the city look as if it was alight with a godly fire. Legends of the First Kings of Jesimae said that they had seen the land where the city now stood and believed the gods meant for them to stay there and create a great nation. Seeing the city now, Aedrik could almost believe that. Aedrian and Calloway joined him on deck, rubbing sleep from their eyes.

"I never get tired of that sight," Aedrian sighed.

"It's too bad you picked Angerona to be your base of operations." Calloway's dry contribution earned an eye roll from both brothers.

"You know why we couldn't come here, Cal. It's too close to eastern territory. We'd never have survived the first *week* of Aedrik's reign."

Aedrik clapped his brother and friend on the back, gesturing for them to precede him below decks once more. "Let's go get the horses and set up shop. I want to give Kilian the biggest surprise of his life."

"Aww, Aed, that's sweet. You're so considerate," Aedrian joked.

"I try," he quipped as he passed them and made his way below, making the sign for luck. Dry laughter followed him and echoed through the tight stairwell.

Chapter 28
The Daeva

It was easier than people thought to inspire loyalty. The Daeva had been doing so for years. No one would dare betray that trust, knowing that their head would not stay on their shoulders for long. More than that, The Daeva demanded a sacrifice of blood or soul when one entered the service. If this oath of fealty was broken, the betrayer would then be subjected to an agonizingly slow and horrific death.

And so, the Daeva proceeded with the plan, supremely confident except for one small thing. The thief, Kilian. He had not made the oath. As a new recruit, he had still been proving himself—a trial period, if you will. Now that he had fled the city and the brothers would stop at nothing to kill him, he was useless to the Daeva as a minion.

Of course, this *could* end up working in the Daeva's favor. If the brothers were distracted by the escaping traitor, they would not be paying attention to the goings on elsewhere.

This was the opportunity the Daeva had been waiting for. Aedrik's asset was as good as captured. They were being transported to the stronghold as the Daeva sipped the wine from the goblet on the table. Within the next week or two they would be here, out of the twins' reach.

Standing, the Daeva walked to the low stone basin in the middle of the chamber. It was filled with crystal clear water. Harsh words from a long-forgotten and long-forbidden language rasped from the wicked throat and the water began to form images within its depths.

A forest, dark and deep, came into focus. Five companions rode horses at a steady pace through the trees. As the Daeva watched, the group broke through the thickest part of the forest and stepped out into a massive clearing. The village of Silvija lay before them, built from and beneath the forest's most ancient trees.

The Daeva smiled, if the gash across its face could be called that. They were almost within grasp. A little more than a week.

Now to wait.

Chapter 29

Emyr

By now, Emyr had figured out one thing for certain: the identity of his most intriguing, crafty, and surprisingly beautiful captor. He had had several moments throughout their travels where he began to piece things together, but after seeing her fight in the woods and the way she was able to manipulate her appearance better than anyone he'd ever seen, he was sure—he'd been captured and tentatively befriended the Red Lady herself, the left hand of His Majesty, "King" Aedrik. He still didn't know her name, no one did. What he couldn't figure out was why Aedrik had decided to kidnap him. There were so many reasons that the Rogue would want him, but none of them really seemed to fit the drastic measures which had clearly been taken.

Glancing at her now across the Great Hall in Silvija, it took a minute for him to find her. Just after they'd been caught in the woods, she'd begun subtly changing her appearance. He understood why. No one living had ever seen the Red Lady's true face and the glamours she'd placed over both of them after their impromptu swim had been minimal at best.

By now, the men who were left of the original fifteen would not be able to recall the face they'd captured her with initially. She had taken the red out of her hair, so it was a dull brown. There was no longer any wave to it, and it fell down to her lower back in a straight waterfall. Her eyes were a grey blue instead of green and she was plumper than she had been. He wondered what she would do to him to make him forget that he knew what she looked like. Emyr wasn't naive enough to believe that he would escape this ordeal unscathed by her. He'd been lucky so far.

As they ate with the woodland people that night, Emyr wondered about her story. What possessed a young girl to hide herself from society and become one of the terrors parents told their young about to keep them from misbehaving? He wanted to make it a point to find out while it was still just the two of them.

Their situation had ironically improved remarkably after the nightmarish battle in the woods. After everything they had gone through together, the Silvijan Guards no longer saw them as captives, stating that standing to fight instead of running was not the mark of an enemy, but a true ally.

Emyr could tell she was happy about this turn of events. When they'd had a rare moment alone, she'd told him that it had been her plan to steal back the horses and supplies so they could continue on their journey. Now, the Chieftain, or *Dasan,* was happily offering them whatever they needed and more. Of course, that was only if they stayed for the memorial of the Fallen, so they had remained the last two nights.

Despite the beauty and prosperity of the small village, these people's lives seemed to revolve around the terrors that resided in the woods. It was considered terrible luck to begin a new journey before those lost on the previous one had been laid to rest. So, they would stay for three days total. An unexpected delay, but Emyr couldn't be mad about sleeping on a real bed for a few nights and giving their wounds a chance to heal.

Besides, while he hadn't been harmed intentionally so far, he had no idea what reception he would get wherever they were going. It wasn't like he could bolt in the middle of the night. She had placed enchantments on him after their dunk in the river so she could track him easily. He wouldn't get much beyond the outer ring of buildings before she caught up with him and he preferred to stay unhobbled by those leafy restraints for as long as possible.

His only consolation was that she'd told him she needed, nay *wanted*, him alive. If she didn't actually want to harm him then he figured he would be safe enough. He couldn't imagine what his father must be thinking right now. If Emyr did not live to succeed the throne, the nobles with the most power would tear each other apart in the mad scramble for the highest seat in the land. Emyr could only imagine his father's white-fisted fury.

Shaking his head and ridding himself of a rather pointless thought process, Emyr responded to the question asked of him by politely deflecting. He had come to realize that in addition to changing her own appearance, the Red Lady had been subtly altering his. Looking in the glass in the washroom earlier had been a bit of a shock. His hair and skin were lighter, like that of a man from the Middle Country, and he was shorter and thinner. Even his nose was larger.

Still, as newcomers in town, they drew quite a bit of attention, and it was making him nervous. At the moment, he couldn't even see her because of the knot of men surrounding her. She was a legend here already, this woman who could best some of their greatest enemies as well as their greatest heroes. The last two days had been filled with request after request from the men to spar with her. Even still healing from her injuries, she had decided to fight, joking that it would be a nice break from her standard morning practice routine. These provincial men didn't stand a chance. She had been hardened at the hands of the best—and least honorable—fighters in the world in the most dangerous place in all of Jesimae, but it had still been highly entertaining to watch.

Emyr found himself attempting to stifle the pride he felt for her every time she taught another brash young man a very valuable lesson in humility. It would not do to get attached to his kidnapper, he knew, but he had not been treated like a captive by her since before they'd fought the desert bandits. When all was said and done though, he still had to arrest her for treason, not to mention—if he could find proof—the many murders she was said to have committed as the Red Lady.

The party raged on, men, women, and children shouting out the names of the Fallen like benedictions to the gods. The earlier ceremony had been a somber affair, but now that the pent-up grief had been let loose, the people were celebrating the lives of those who had given theirs for the safety of the village. Songs were already being composed about the Great Battle at the Ruins.

It was with some chagrin that Emyr noticed "the Strangers from the West" featured prominently in these sagas. His companion had given them false names. These people would never know who they had really taken in, but he had not felt like a hero after that battle and hated being mentioned as their voices lifted in joy and gratitude.

It didn't really matter. After tomorrow they would be gone from these people's lives forever. Emyr pushed through the crowd until he found her at the center.

He wanted to find a moment alone with her—to hopefully get some information and just have a few minutes not surrounded by prying eyes. He had gotten used to the comfort and solitude of traveling in such a small company.

Chapter 30
Ashdan

Ashdan smiled and laughed in all the right places. She was a good actress from years of hiding her identity, but she was not used to people treating her like a hero. It made her highly uncomfortable because she definitely wasn't. She knew that. Her brothers definitely knew that. Emyr had been kind, but she knew he was very much aware that he was still her captive. For some reason, the fact that he knew her true face didn't bother her as much as it had in the beginning.

She had to be careful.

She could feel herself getting used to his presence. It would be incredibly stupid of her to let her guard down around him. He was no longer bound, and she had allowed him to reclaim his weapons. For all she knew, he was planning to kill her while she slept so she couldn't track him if he escaped.

The young men surrounding her were babies and she tried her best to deflect their admiration elsewhere. They were currently jockeying for the places closest to her, as if she would want *any* of them near her. Luckily, tomorrow she and Emyr would be gone. In fact, she planned on leaving just before dawn.

Another song was struck up nearby. *The Ballad of the Great Battle in the Ruins* rang out for what seemed like the fortieth time that night. She was just looking for an escape route, so she didn't have to hear about her supposed heroics once more when she spotted Emyr making his way towards her.

"If you gentlemen will excuse me; I need to have a quick conversation with my friend." She tried not to laugh at the crestfallen faces of the young warriors. As soon as she stepped out of their circle, a veritable hoard of young women filtered in to take her place, many glaring in her direction. Emyr laughed at that as she took his elbow, and they made their way to the edge of the village square.

"I think you've made an equal amount of enemies here as you have admirers."

She rolled her eyes. "People are ridiculous. Enemies I can handle, but I'm not a hero."

"No, I don't suppose you are, considering the things you've done."

She looked up sharply at him, then sighed. "I suppose I should have expected you would figure it out eventually. You're smarter than the rumors give you credit for, you know."

She could see he didn't know whether to take that as a compliment or insult. Good. She needed to keep him on his toes around her.

"So, since I've figured out your identity, do I get to know your name? Or should I just call you Lady?"

She laughed at that and relented, figuring it couldn't hurt to lay it all out now. "Ashdan."

"Their sister. Interesting. I'd heard rumors that Ashdan was dead." His eyes glinted in the darkness, and she refused to acknowledge what that did to her insides. "I bet I'm one of very few people who know that."

She nodded, slightly uncomfortable, but telling herself to calm down. He had nowhere to go, and it wasn't the end of the world if everyone knew that the Red Lady was actually the Rogue's younger sister. It had just been an added layer of mystery around the persona she had created.

They reached the room they'd been given in the *Dasan's* home and entered, both lost in their private thoughts. It was small and quaint with simply carved wooden furniture. A fire crackled merrily in the clay hearth. They sat beside each other on the bed they'd been alternating use of since they arrived. If the people thought they were together, so much the better. It added another layer to their ruse.

Since the curtains were drawn and the door locked, she allowed their features to morph back to their natural shapes. No sense wasting magic. He was looking at her with a strange expression in his eyes.

"I can't tell you why if that's what you're waiting for. I wish I could trust you fully, but for obvious reasons I can't. All I will say is that we have no intention of harming you in any way and you *will* be returned home safely as soon as we get what we need."

He cocked his head at her use of the word *need,* but his expression didn't change. Had she given too much away even with that little slip? It would have been easier to tell him it was all about money.

No, that was just a nice little bonus of having something that the richest man in the country wanted back desperately.

This was about survival.

She worried that he would start to figure it out if she continued on the subject, but he seemed to have the politician's knack for knowing when to drop a subject because he suddenly changed tactics completely. He stepped up and faced her by the hearth.

"Tell me about growing up with your brothers. What was that like?"

That wasn't what she was expecting. What should she tell him, if anything? He was standing very close. She started sweating. Was it hot in here?

Stop it, Ash. You are an assassin. Get your shit together.

Her family. Right. Talking about them would definitely cool her off.

"Well...as you may know already, my father was Rogue before Aedrik. He was..." she trailed off, not knowing quite what to say. "He had a darkness in him. My mother wasn't much better, in fact, she was worse, but the twins and I were able to scrape by. With each other's help of course."

"Of course. So, I was wondering…and I'm only asking this because no one will probably ever have a chance like this again…"

She sighed, knowing what came next.

"…What made you become—"

"The Red Lady?" she finished for him.

He nodded, his expression rabidly curious.

"I mean, you don't have to tell me, but there has to be a reason, right? Someone doesn't just wake up one day and do those things."

Those things. She had never considered that what she was doing was wrong. Sure, her methods were ill-advised by most people's standards, but she had *saved* countless lives by ridding them of the monsters that plagued her city and wanted to cause dissent where there didn't need to be.

She didn't dare admit to him that she actually enjoyed taking their lives, but maybe she could make him see *why* she did it.

"My father was a terrible man. Not just a criminal. I'm a criminal. I admit that freely. And a killer. But Damian was *evil*. He didn't think anything of harming children—even his own."

Emyr's face grew darker as she spoke, but she continued.

"One night, when we were much younger, he…he nearly killed all three of us. We were scrappy at that age, but couldn't defend ourselves against a fully grown man, let alone the King of Thieves.

He'd gotten hopped up on the Red Flower. It was all the rage in Angerona at the time. Mother actually tried to intervene. She'd never done that before.

A month later, tales of the Red Lady began to spread because I needed the thing that turned people into monsters—that hideous drug—to be eradicated. It took ten years and all three of us, but eventually we stopped the spread and put our father where he belonged.

When Aedrik took over, we didn't allow people to make the connection between the new Rogue's younger sister and the Red Lady. It helped my reputation build that much faster."

"But you got rid of the Red Flower. Now, what you're doing is still a crime."

"And what those people are doing isn't? Their method of rebelling against my brother is to wreak havoc on the *city* without challenging him outright. I'm keeping the peace."

She could argue the merits of her actions all day and not convince him. She shouldn't have even tried. She knew she was a criminal, murderer, and assassin. That didn't mean she wasn't doing *any* good, but it was unlikely that he would ever see it that way.

"Why didn't you just report those men to the law?"

She almost choked on the laugh that threatened to escape.

"Many of those people *were* and still are the law. Corruption travels higher than you think, Your Highness."

They were standing closer now, glaring at each other. She was sure she'd just ruined whatever tentative truce they had built over the time they had been traveling, but it had felt so good to tell someone the truth for once.

He seemed to sink into himself, and his expression went blank once again as he reached out a hand to caress her cheek. She didn't pull away though she knew she should. He was so close now she could smell the delicious combination of sun and sea he always seemed to carry, and she swayed with longing.

After a minute or two, he said distractedly, "I suppose it's kind of like when we defended Jesimae from invaders last year. They were trying to harm innocent people. I've killed. I won't pretend I haven't."

Ashdan could scarcely believe what he was saying.

"I can try to understand, Ashdan, but know that if you are ever caught, I can do nothing to save you."

His voice pled with her not to let that happen and his hand slid to the back of her head, twisting in her hair. She couldn't breathe. So close. His lips were barely a breath away. It was like being starving and seeing a feast on the other side of an open window.

Ashdan waited breathlessly for him to close the distance—for his lips to take hers in the kind of kiss they'd both been craving. Personal morals be damned. But she realized in a moment of shock that he wouldn't.

He was waiting for her to meet *him* the rest of the way. To make sure this was what they *both* wanted. And she wanted to. Oh, how she wanted to. It wouldn't take much. He was so close, if she breathed in deep, her chest would press against his. She hovered on the edge of indecision, staring into his darkened hungry eyes.

She found herself swaying forward without conscious thought. And his lips touched hers. Just the barest of touches, so light she could almost believe it wasn't there at all. But it was there, and she was already gasping for more.

She couldn't take that last step—couldn't close the gap. If she gave up that kind of control to him…

His words had been along the lines of what she had been expecting. It seemed as if he was willing to overlook their differences if the stifled groan that escaped him and sank into her bones was any indication.

But she'd drugged and kidnapped him.

And he'd be *king* one day.

This could go absolutely nowhere.

Okay. Time to disengage.

She stepped back, turning to face the flames, hoping he'd think the flush in her cheeks was due to the heat from the fire. He let his hand fall to his side, eyes searching her profile before he blew out an unsteady breath and went to lay down.

He stared up at the ceiling, face expressionless and jaw clenched. *She* attempted to get her heartrate under control and after a moment, she lay down on the sleeping pad set before the hearth.

They were silent for a time. Wishing they were closer. She didn't dare look at him. Her will power stood no chance if those eyes ensnared her once again. A new rendition of their heroic deeds filtered in through the night air, making them both cringe. She wrapped herself in the soft blanket and turned away.

After a moment, he sat up and called her name.

"Ash. This is ridiculous. There's plenty of room on this bed. There's no need for you to sleep on the floor."

She rolled over and met his eyes at last. It was a bad idea. But the floor was stone and she knew it would be a while before they found comfortable beds again.

"Fine."

She stood and stalked over to the bed. His eyes left her hers, but not her body. Every part of her lit up as they moved over her curves.

Nameless One, save me, she thought. The man was going to make her lose all the strength in her legs. When he pulled back the covers for her to climb in, she sat tentatively on the edge of the mattress. He didn't speak, but tilted his head as if to say, *Come here.*

She slid closer and lay down, facing him.

He laid down again close enough she could once again feel his breath. She couldn't take it anymore.

Reaching behind his head, she grabbed him and pulled his lips to hers. His pleased surprise gave way very quickly to desperate hunger that matched hers. She curled her body around him, her leg wrapping around his hip. She could feel every muscle even through the clothes they both still wore.

She was reaching down to his belt to relieve him of said clothes, when a loud crash sounded and raucous laughter filtered in through curtained, but open window. They jumped apart though it was clear from the ensuing noise that the revelers were just getting rowdy.

"Ash," he said, "you can put those down."

She hadn't even realized that she'd pulled out two knives at the sound of the crash. She sheathed them, but pulled the covers over her and turned away. What had she been thinking?

"We should get some sleep."

He didn't move for a moment, but eventually settled down—farther away this time.

"If that's what you want."

"It's what I want," she snapped.

He didn't answer and pretty soon his breathing grew slow and even with sleep.

It would be a long time before Ashdan's eyes drooped closed. She couldn't get the way his hands and lips felt on her body out of her mind. The way that soft groan had let her know he wanted this as much as he did. She fought with herself for hours until finally, sleep came to put her out of her misery.

What seemed like seconds later, a rooster crowed with the false dawn, and she opened her eyes to find the fire had died as they slept. In the barest blue light of the frigid pre-dawn morning, Ashdan gazed upon the face of the peacefully sleeping Prince. It didn't matter that the shape of his cheek bones broke her heart. Or that he kissed like he had a completely different occupation. Or that his skin was warm and soft, and she wanted to experience all of it pressed to all of hers. Nope.

Her priorities were once again set straight.

She hoped.

Chapter 31
Aedrian

It was a small miracle that Kilian would not be arriving until today. They'd had plenty of time to lay their traps and fail safes. If one didn't spring, another would. The beauty of being one of the most powerful criminals in the country was that people would do anything to get in Aedrian's good graces.

They'd only enlisted a select few, handpicked by Aedrik's Lieutenant that oversaw the Capital, but it would be more than enough to find the spineless vermin that had slithered on to the ship now coming into dock. Now that everything was in place though, it would just be the three of them who would take Kilian down.

This was personal.

Reports had been coming in for the last two days from along the ship's route. No one had seen or heard of anyone jumping ship early. Someone *had* witnessed a man matching Kilian's description board the ship and with the information they'd gathered in Ryton, they were almost entirely sure they would find him on this ship.

Of course, there was always the off chance that he'd somehow managed to evade them completely and was now happily sailing away from the country with his stolen horse and supplies, but Aedrian wasn't in the habit of underestimating his opponents and could be fairly certain that this wasn't the case.

In fact, Aedrik would sometimes give him a hard time for overestimating their opponents' capabilities. Aedrian would always respond with, "We were underestimated once. Look where it got *us*." That usually shut his brother up.

Now, Aedrian felt confident in their preparations and settled into his perch to watch the large, weathered ship come in. Enhancing his sight a bit with magic, Aedrian could just make out the faces of those on the top deck. He scanned, hungrily, for that familiar face. The chance to pay Kilian back for what he'd done to Cal was finally within grasp and there was no way he was letting that go.

After several moments of fruitless searching, he spotted his target. The lanky hair was unkempt, and he looked green with sea illness. One of the crew members stuffed his bag in his hands and shoved him toward the area where the exit ramp would be as soon as they docked.

Aedrian tried to read his expression across the ever-decreasing distance. He did not look happy. Good. If only he knew how much worse things were about to get. On second thought, Aedrian was more than happy to keep that little morsel to himself for a while longer.

When the ship pulled into the harbor, Aedrian found himself vibrating with excitement. Kilian was laughed off the ship by the crew. He cast a belligerent glare back at the men, but stumbled on to dry land, looking relieved.

Aedrian was glad to see that it wasn't just them who found Kilian's false bravado to be laughable. He followed on the rooftops above as Kilian made his way to an inn close to the wharf. Somehow, he bullied the innkeeper into giving him one of the nicer rooms before disappearing inside.

Aedrian settled in for a long wait. He supposed they could spring their trap now, but they preferred to work under the cover of night. Besides, it was more satisfying to catch a man when his guard was at its lowest. The surprise on their face was always particularly gratifying. After the trip he'd had, Kilian would sleep quite soundly tonight. That's when they would strike.

In the meantime, Aedrian enjoyed the sunset and counted down the minutes until his retribution would be complete.

Chapter 32
Aedrik

It was late, but the docks of Tsifira were still teaming with life. Aedrik loved coming to this city and marveling at how different it was from Angerona. Even the wealthy people were down at the docks here in all their finery. The area was brightly lit. To a normal thief, that would be a slight hindrance, but to Aedrik and his two companions, it only meant that the shadows were that much darker where they did exist.

It was through these very shadows that they moved—as though night itself sped between the sand and pastel-colored buildings. He could sense his brother high above the lights, leaping across the rooftops. Calloway flanked him on the ground as they found the perfect spot to scale the inn. Aedrik had charmed a very helpful maid earlier that day into feeding them information about Kilian's movements. Currently, he was fast asleep and snoring in his room.

He grabbed hold of the top of a ground floor window and hoisted himself up onto the low awning, Calloway following close behind. Kilian's room on the top floor forced them to take a circuitous route up the building. When they couldn't find hand holds, their knives were more than sufficient as a substitute.

The night air coming off the sea cooled the sweat beading on their foreheads. When Aedrik glanced up to the roof, he could no longer see his brother's silhouette, meaning he was probably already inside, disarming the target.

A final push and he sat on the windowsill. Looking inside, he spotted Kilian sprawled naked on the bed. He wrinkled his nose in disgust. The man was filthy. How he could go to bed in that state, Aedrik would never know. He decided to leave a generous tip for the maid who would have to clean those sheets and hoped they could force Kilian into some clothes before running off with him.

Unsurprisingly, the window was already unlocked. *Thanks, Aedrian.* He reached down and gave Calloway a hand, pulling the large blonde man into the room noiselessly. A quick look around revealed the glint of a curved blade swinging in the deep shadow of the doorway. Aedrik nodded to his brother, waited until Calloway was in position, then sank out of the moonlit path in front of the window.

A quick flex of powers slammed the window shut with a bang. Kilian jerked awake, reaching for the weapons that were no longer there.

"You know; you really should learn to keep your weapons in less obvious places." Aedrian stepped forward, still swinging his weapon. It glinted and flashed as it passed from one hand to another. The other man froze, squinting in the dim light.

Calloway helpfully dropped a log on the coals of the fire. The room lit with an eerie red glow. Kilian's face paled, seeing the three of them. Aedrik grinned and gestured with his blade.

"Get dressed."

When Kilian hesitated, Aedrian took another step forward, blade still spinning around his hands. The terrified man crammed his legs into his trousers and yanked a shirt over his head. Calloway tossed him his empty sword belt, but he didn't catch it in time. It smacked him upside the face.

Aedrik couldn't help the chuckle that escaped him. The man was pathetic and deserved to die, but they could still make use of him. When they returned to Angerona, he would make an excellent example, having stirred such trouble beforehand.

While Kilian attempted to stammer apologies and explanations, Aedrian had tucked his beloved blade back into his belt and was now twining something else through his fingers. As they watched, it grew. Aedrik realized it was a leaf. Kilian looked confused, then terrified when Aedrian moved still closer. Aedrik and Calloway moved in as well, cornering him against the bed.

Aedrian reached out, grabbing his lank hair. He threw him to the floor in the center of the room. Aedrik was a little surprised at the force of his brother's rage. He was usually so reserved, but this time he threw Kilian to the ground and began beating him mercilessly.

"As much as I'd like to beat the life out of you right here, scum, I don't want to be rude to the other kind patrons of this top-notch establishment. Besides—" Kick.

"You—"

Kick.

"Are—"

Kick.

"Coming with us." *Kick.*

"Alive."

Aedrik pulled Kilian's hands behind his back, then took the expanded foliage from his brother's clenched fists and allowed it to wrap itself around Kilian's wrists. The ends met and attached as if there had never been a break. Kilian pulled at his bonds in vain. They only tightened, the more he pulled.

"Handy little trick, brother."

Aedrian shrugged, his eyes still sparking with anger and tossed more than enough coin on the bed for the maid and to cover the room.

They decided to exit through the front door and parade Kilian in front of anyone who might still be awake at this hour. Calloway grabbed him by the scruff of the neck. On the way out, Kilian's head accidentally slammed against the door jam.

"Oops," said Calloway. Aedrik shoved them all out the door, bringing up the rear with Kilian's belongings. When they made it to the bottom floor—not without a couple of useless attempts at escape on Kilian's part—they were pleasantly surprised to see a good-sized crowd still carousing and drinking. They fell silent when they spotted the bound man and his three captors.

Aedrik stepped out in front of their group, swinging Kilian's pack nonchalantly onto his shoulder.

"This man is wanted for heinous crimes in Angerona. We'll be taking him back where he belongs now. He won't bother you folks again."

Several people still looked worried, but the ones who recognized Aedrik and his brother gave them imperceptible nods of respect. The innkeeper stepped forward, looking as if he were about to protest, but Calloway intercepted him, placing a gold coin in his hand.

"For your trouble."

His expression didn't change until he caught sight of the insignia on Calloway's sword—that of an Elite Guardsman. The older man backed away and ushered them out politely, offering food and water skins for their journey. Thinking it was probably a good idea to take him up on the offer as long as it stood, they left the inn laden down with extra food, water, and their prisoner effectively silenced by a quick flex of Aedrik's powers.

Aedrian let out a small whoop when they entered the quiet streets, punching his fist into the air. Blue sparks erupted around him for a split second.

"Since you're so energized, brother, I'll let you light the way."

They strolled away from the inn, deeper into the city, sinking back into the shadows once again as the fires along Aedrian's arms went out.

Chapter 33

Ashdan

The air was crisp and cool as they wondered through the sleeping village. A fine mist coated everything, making their stay in this idyllic place like a fond dream. Ashdan gathered her cloak tighter around herself and motioned for Emyr to pick up the pace.

They exited Silvija without a sound, leaving the people in peaceful sleep, unaware of who exactly they had been hosting. It was for the better. That kind of knowledge would only put them in danger and Ashdan thought it better that they remain in their utopian bubble as long as possible.

Another day and a half of traveling took them across the Tamesis river—thankfully by bridge this time—out of the woods, and into the foothills of the Licean Mountains. The vegetation grew more and more sparse the higher they went until camping under a copse of trees was no longer an option.

The first night out in the open made Ashdan extremely nervous. She kept the fire small and smokeless, staying up all night to keep watch despite the wards she had placed around camp. She regretted it the next morning as she dragged her body through her daily exercises with each of her weapons.

She and Emyr didn't talk much as they traveled. The talk they had had back in Silvija hung around them in a thick cloud of tension. He was the Crown Prince of Jesimae, would one day be King, and she was the woman taking justice into her own hands and murdering his citizens. It didn't matter that he could sympathize with her reasoning.

According to the law, he was supposed to have her arrested and hanged. Something like that would put a damper on any relationship, kidnapping aside. The other kind of tension also hung around them, but she didn't even let her mind go there. Remembering their argument helped her reorient herself. The lines no longer blurred. He was her captive, and she had a mission to complete.

Ashdan knew they were getting close to her mother's fortress, Sonneillon, when what little vegetation there was began to wither then disappeared altogether. Emyr noticed this and made a comment about it one morning.

"My mother practices magic that draws energy from the earth. Unfortunately, it also kills it if she takes too much."

"You're taking me to meet your mother?"

She didn't miss the cheeky grin on his face—it was the first she'd seen from him in days—but chose to ignore it.

"Yeah. That reminds me."

She pulled out the ties they hadn't used since being attacked in the desert. This time, she lightly bound his hands and placed one over his eyes. The brush of his skin against hers sent shivers through her body and he'd gone unnaturally still. She kept talking out of self-preservation.

"Standard procedure. Only her children know how to get to Sonneillon, and she would like to keep it that way."

"Oh, sure. Of course."

The dry tone of his voice made her roll her eyes.

"I'm also hoping she'll be able to tell us what's been going on with your skin."

Emyr self-consciously pulled the collar of his shirt closed over his mottled skin, struggling with his bound hands. Ashdan laughed at him.

"Don't worry, Your Highness, your pretty, flawless skin will be back to normal soon."

He snorted.

"At least it hasn't done that strange bubbling thing since I completely dried off from our dunk in the river."

Their banter was cut short as they passed into the valley that would ultimately lead to the fortress. Even Emyr noticed the shift from behind his blindfold. The darkness that embraced them and all sounds of life faded away.

"We're getting close, aren't we?"

He tried to speak quietly, but that lack of nature here meant his voice echoed off the rocks ahead, and he almost choked on the last two words in his haste to return to quiet.

"Mother doesn't really like visitors. Especially since father's death. The entrance to her fortress tends to send the desired message."

A clear stream traveled past them in the opposite direction as if fleeing form Lorraen's foul and intemperate moods. Ashdan sighed and reminded herself that this was the safest place to be until her brothers got her word that they'd received the information they needed.

The valley grew darker with each branch she took through the mountains. Their massive height nearly blocked the late day sun completely. She was forced to light a small torch in order to see where they were going.

They traveled ever upward, along narrow paths and canyon walls that forced them single file. The horses plodded along, trusting Ashdan implicitly.

They were on a particularly perilous path, getting close, when they heard an otherworldly hiss from above. Emyr's face paled beneath his blindfold, and he reached for the sword she had removed from his belt. They both immediately recognized that sound. Their wounds from the last encounter with the creatures from the ruins had scarred quickly thanks to the Silvijan's Healer, but the terror and bone deep chill remained.

Ashdan looked up and saw a creature not dissimilar to the ones they had fought in the forest lurking twenty feet above their heads. It stared down at them, unmoving, as though it was waiting for a command.

"Ashdan. Let me out of my bindings so I can help fight them off."

"No."

"No?"

"They're not attacking. They're just—they're just watching. Guarding...oh, Mom!"

"She's using them as guard dogs?"

"This is a new development."

They picked their way carefully along the path, Ashdan keeping her weapons at the ready, but the creatures never moved from their perches on the rocks above. A few hundred feet up the path, Ashdan spotted the mark she'd been looking for. A small overhang jutted over their path and threw everything underneath deep into blackness. As soon as they were directly underneath, Ashdan turned them sharply to the right, headed into the mountain.

Chapter 34
Emyr

Emyr could no longer tell where they were by paying attention to the light filtering through the binding around his eyes. Pitch darkness surrounded them and there was a feeling of damp closeness that reminded him of the catacombs underneath the Palace at home. The air grew colder the farther they went. Pretty soon, they were both huddling as far into their cloaks as possible.

"Any chance this place has a fire going?"

His chattering teeth and voice echoing off the walls sounded wrong, too loud, but it confirmed his guess that they were in a tunnel. When Ashdan responded, it was so quiet, he almost missed it.

"She certainly makes it hard for intruders, but we're almost there."

"You know, you use way too many euphemisms and understatements when talking about your mother." He lowered his voice to match hers. "I'm starting to think she's going to take me out with one glance."

He heard her soft chuckle.

"It's been known to happen. Just follow my lead."

Great. Was there anyone in her family who was *not* a homicidal maniac?

"I think you're enjoying this too much."

"You're not the first person to accuse me of that."

"No, I suppose not." As his sentence trailed off, he felt the sound lose itself in a much larger space. They had exited the tunnel. He heard her pull her horse close to his and, seconds later, the blindfold was removed from his eyes. Torches around the room were lit with an eerie blue firelight that could not have been natural.

The room seemed to be some kind of large atrium or throne room. Heavy curtains blocked something from view on the side opposite the tunnel. An ornate chair sat empty on a dais. Three much larger tunnels than the one they'd just exited branched off from the room.

As they took it all in, a lantern filled with that same blue fire travelled closer and a thin man with a rat like face carried it. His footsteps were nearly soundless. They almost missed him as they dismounted; Ashdan helped Emyr as he struggled with the bonds still tying his hands. The man stopped in front of them. He barely glanced at Emyr, but bowed deeply to Ashdan.

"Your lady mother is glad you've arrived safely. She will greet you in her chambers."

Emyr's eyebrows rose at the reference to Ashdan's "lady mother." This woman must be a piece of work to put on airs as if she were a noble. Clearly, this man knew exactly who he was, but it didn't seem to matter. His loyalty was with the mistress of the house apparently, not the Crown Prince of Jesimae. If nothing else, this journey had certainly been eye-opening in a way the Royal Progress had not.

Another servant came out of nowhere and led their horses away. Baela nickered at him and he glanced back, slightly worried. *Ashdan* may have treated him well, but he was still a prisoner. He hoped that man knew how to treat a fine horse such as his. The rat-faced man led them back down the hallway he'd come from. No words were spoken. Ashdan put a hand under his elbow and guided him along like a true prisoner. And though he knew why, it still hurt. Over the weeks they'd been traveling, she hadn't done that even once and he liked to think she was keeping up appearances for her mother and not reverting back to how it had been that first night in the desert.

The hallway they passed through was wide and tall enough for four men to ride abreast. It made him wonder how long it had taken to carve this place from the stone of the mountain. Given the smoothness of the walls and floor, Emyr suspected magic had been involved.

Speaking of magic...

The further they walked down the passage, the thicker the air became until they had to physically push to take the next step. Emyr noticed that every step they took through the charged air stripped them a little more of the disguises they had resumed after leaving Silvija. His mottled skin started to hum and shift again as it had after their flight through the river. He glanced over at Ashdan in alarm.

Her face was set in an angry pout. Finally, it seemed as though she'd had enough. He watched sweat begin to bead on her forehead and the now visible markings on her skin glowed blue. It was suddenly a lot easier to move. Emyr's skin stopped its uncomfortable shifting, but retained its strange spots. It was like there was something just beneath the surface, trying to find its way out.

They trudged their way along what remained of the corridor to stand in front of a set of impressively carved double doors depicting entwined serpents devouring one another. It was impossible to tell where the line of doomed creatures began or ended, and Emyr wanted to turn back the way they came. The hairs on his arms and neck stood straight up at the ominous image and the power emanating from the room beyond.

The servant, who hadn't seemed affected by Lorraen's spell in the slightest, knocked politely and announced the visitors. A rich feminine voice called from beyond the thick wood, "Enter!" and the doors swung open of their own accord.

They were greeted with the sight of an opulently furnished chamber. Low, plush couches formed a semi-circle around a beautiful blown glass table. The room was draped in rich reds, golds, and purples. It looked as though Ashdan's mother had collected the finest things from around the world and put them all together in this one room. He wondered how a woman who stayed shut in her impenetrable castle managed to gather so many fine things, but he supposed being married to the Rogue and mother of the next had its perks.

As for the woman, she stood to the far left, looking out over a splendid view of the mountain range and beyond. She was the same height as her daughter, but had long jet-black hair like her sons. As full Elymas, she had glyphs covering every inch of visible skin, including ones that inched their way onto her cheekbones and chin.

But instead of black, they were the same dark red as the clothing she wore. Though her face was unlined, her deep-set black eyes held the weight of her years and experiences. Lorraen du Sonneillon was a fascinating and terrifying creature. There was no warmth in her gaze as it landed upon her daughter.

Chapter 35
The Daeva

The Daeva stared at the pair standing by the doorway. It took a moment to remember that the woman by the double doors was their daughter. It had been years since they'd spoken to one another. Many things had changed since then. That Ashdan and her brothers thought this was a safe place to stash their prize was a testament to how long it had been.

Lorraen schooled cold features into something resembling a smile. "Ashdan. Welcome. I'm sure you are tired after your journey. We will speak tomorrow." A nod to the servant hovering in the background dismissed her visitors. There was no point in wasting time with pleasantries.

Ashdan's face didn't change, but Lorraen could sense her confusion at the gruff dismissal. Years ago, the old Lorraen might have stopped herself from what she was about to do, but those human bonds no longer held any weight with the Daeva. And that was who she was now.

Human connection, love, was weakness. There was no room for weakness if one desired power. And wasn't that the only desire worth pursuing? Wasn't that the only thing that provided any satisfaction?

Lorraen waited until the doors shut completely. Left alone again, the Daeva turned back to the view of the South. Now all that was left was the waiting.

"Come to me, my son. It will be an...eventful family reunion."

Somewhere below came the sound of the doors to a metal cage slamming shut. The shouting began. The Daeva swayed contentedly to the rhythm of the screams as they began to drift throughout the fortress.

The sounds made *Lorraen* pause for a second. A surge in the stone heart within the pale breast caused long tapering hands to clench into fists, but the motherly instinct was crushed in a moment—gone before it had a chance to take root once more.

Chapter 36
Aedrik

Aedrik watched Kilian with narrowed eyes. He was curled into a ball, sleeping as if he didn't have a care in the world. He found it ironic that while their captive slept like a small child, neither he nor his brother could sleep. They had left the capital hours ago, but Aedrik still couldn't shake the feeling that something was terribly wrong. Could it be something to do with Kilian? They had taken every precaution. The man wasn't going anywhere without their say-so.

Earlier that day they'd bound Kilian by blood to Aedrian. If anything happened to him, Kilian would be in utter agony until he either rectified the situation or killed himself. Aedrian had protested during the entire process, arguing that Kilian should be tied to Aedrik since he was the Rogue and therefore more valuable, but Aedrik had shot him down.

He tended to act recklessly. If something happened to him, as it was bound to one day, he needed to know that his second in command had the protection he needed to step into his place. But he hadn't done it for purely unselfish reasons—Aedrik had no desire whatsoever to be bonded to the man who had been his greatest threat up until a few weeks ago. It was kind of an asshole move on Aedrik's part to foist the burden onto his twin, but he'd never pretended to be a good person.

Calloway bounded into the clearing where they had camped, signaling the all-clear when he noticed that they were not asleep. Aedrik ignored his curious glances at the sight of both brothers awake and alert earlier than planned and went to take Calloway's place on watch.

The low murmur of conversation between Aedrian and Calloway faded as he pulled his weapon and moved into the trees. The night was cool and clear, with Magena Moon Goddess shining at her full strength. A small adjustment to his vision and Aedrik could see to the edge of the thinning trees. Beyond them, the Great Plains opened up to the Eastern half of Jesimae.

They were in enemy territory here and no precaution was too great. The Tamesis River separated his territory from the Daeva's, dividing the country in half, and Aedrik hoped sticking to within a few miles of the black waters would provide them a decent enough escape route should they need it.

Footsteps behind him alerted him to his brother's presence. Aedrian's voice whispered out of the darkness,

"I know we said we were going to stop in Aahva to exchange horses before going back home, but I can't shake the feeling that we need to go north—"

"—To see Mom. I know. I feel the same way. At first, I thought it was something to do with Kilian, but we've got the bastard locked down. No. Something's wrong with Mom. We can't leave Ashdan to try and help her by herself. You know what she's like when she gets out of control."

"Right. So, we continue north after Aahva. We're still farther east than I would like. We'll have to be extremely careful as we go on."

"You don't have to tell me twice. Try to go get some sleep. Morning will be here soon enough."

Aedrian made a face at him, but left willingly enough. The benefit of having a twin was that one tended to know when the other needed to be left alone.

The night was peaceful and quiet. Knowing there was no immediate danger, Aedrik decided to try and follow the feeling that wouldn't go away. If he followed it far enough, maybe he could find out more about what was wrong. His connection to his mother and sister wasn't as intense as it was with his twin, but they were blood. There was always a way.

He shut his eyes and let his magic fill him. Whenever he did this, he imagined the magic to be a searing, bubbling liquid that spread through his veins and set his whole body alight. When he was pulsing with the energy, he cast out into the distance for the minds of his mother and sister.

Easier said than done. Not only were they both several days ride away, but both women were exceptionally skilled at shielding their mental signature. He gripped tight to the uneasy feeling and used it as a tether to connect him to their minds. Working his way along it, he hit several snags as though someone was intentionally blocking him from reaching his family. Not. Going. To. Happen.

Alarm bells started to go off and he pushed harder. Aedrik knew his physical form was probably drenched in sweat now, but his mind was miles away, almost to Sonneillon. A bit more effort and he felt the cold stone of his mother's fortress surround him. His mind collided with his mother's and glanced off, ricocheting into the ether before he could get himself under control again. He grabbed hold of the tether again and worked his way back until he was once again within the walls of Sonneillon. There was no penetrating Lorraen's shields, so he decided to try Ashdan. When he reached her, he found her equally closed off, but in a way he couldn't place. Almost as if she was doing it by accident. As if *she* was not the one shielding her mind at all.

The shock of that realization snapped Aedrik harshly back into his body. He clambered off of the rock he'd been perched on, dislodging the curious squirrel that had taken up residence in his lap.

It glared reproachfully at him, and he wondered exactly how long his mental journey had taken. Animals were usually Aedrian's thing. The sky was growing light. It had to have been at least three hours because the magic radiating from his body had seeped into the earth and lit up the whole clearing in a soft blue glow.

He raced back to camp, suddenly afraid that he'd been gone too long. His brother, Calloway, and Kilian were all fast asleep around the smoldering embers, but Aedrian sensed his panicked state even in sleep and bolted upright. They looked at each other, hardly needing words.

Aedrian began to pack up and Aedrik moved to wake the others. He hastily explained their change in plans. Kilian looked torn between misery and hope. Delaying their return to Angerona, meant a delay in his punishment. On the other hand, being dragged on a cross country journey in hostile territory as a captive was almost worse than just getting things over with.

Calloway just nodded and moved to help Aedrian. In less than ten minutes, their entire campsite was packed up and they had erased all traces of their presence. The brothers dropped the wards they had placed around the clearing, they all mounted their horses, and set off at a swift trot toward the small plains town of Aahva.

Chapter 37
Aedrian

It was another day before they reached Aahva. They rode hard, only stopping to water the horses with what they had managed to pack into their water skins. It made everyone nervous to travel deeper into the Daeva's territory, but Aahva was northeast of their campsite, and they were forced to leave the relative shelter of the Tamesis' banks for the open plains. By the time they approached Aahva's outskirts, the sun had long since fallen behind the horizon and the temperature had dropped significantly.

Aedrian was wishing fervently right now that he had his sister's ability to disguise them. The most he'd been able to do was lighten his and Aedrik's hair to a chestnut brown instead of their usual jet black and Aedrik had nearly taken off their heads trying to change their facial structure.

In the end, they had stuck with the lighter hair and Calloway had tied a cloth around his head to prevent anyone from seeing his shocking blonde hair. Between these changes and the fact that they were filthy with dust from the road, Aedrian hoped it would be enough to let them pass through town unrecognized.

There was no wall surrounding Aahva. It sat at the top of a steep plateau in the middle of the plains. The inhabitants could see threats coming for miles. Aedrian was sure they had been watching them approach since before sunset. They finally rounded the last switchback to the top of the plateau and entered the town. It was still early enough that lanterns were lit, shining brightly out of almost every window. People passed, some eyeing them curiously, but most simply going about their business.

This was clearly not a town that was staunchly in the grips of either Rogue. Those places often had a warier air about them. Aahva seemed open and carefree.

They made their way to the center where the low mud-brick buildings grew a little taller and a little wider. When they at last spotted an inn, Aedrian's tired shoulders slumped in relief. He was prepared to rough it as much as he needed to get to his family sooner, but he was glad he didn't have to tonight. Sleeping in a real bed was a gift most people took for granted.

He never would again.

When they shuffled wearily to the bar to ask for a room, the innkeeper didn't even bat an eye. Once they handed over the money, he handed over a room key and told them to get some supper before the maid took it off the hearth for the night. Aedrian tried not to glare at Kilian, who sat across from him at the table.

In order to not arouse suspicion, they had to treat him as a traveling companion here, but Aedrian found it hard to stomach eating at the same table as the man who had nearly killed Calloway and his brother on multiple occasions.

He couldn't imagine how Cal or Aedrik felt, but they seemed to be taking everything in stride. In fact, Calloway had told Aedrian earlier that it was pointless holding on to his own anger at Kilian because Aedrian was angry enough for the both of them.

They all finished eating in silence, then made their way upstairs to fall exhaustedly into their respective beds. Kilian was relegated to sleeping on the floor as Aedrik refused to share a bed with him. Aedrian wanted to point out that his brother was being childish, but he felt that would be a little hypocritical given his own thoughts at dinner. Instead, he allowed Cal to pull him tight against his lean chest and relished the feeling of finally being able to embrace the man the way he'd always wanted.

When they woke in the morning, Aedrian made his way out into the town square to see who he could charm or bribe into exchanging horses. If he was unsuccessful, they wouldn't hesitate to steal them, but it was better not to attract the attention of the Daeva while in their territory.

The first man he tried took one look at their horses and told him they weren't worth half of one of his. It was true. The Aahvans were exceptional horse breeders. Trying to obtain one of their horses was a costly endeavor. Just when he was starting to think they may have to resort to theft, Aedrian encountered a very smiley young woman who agreed to loan them her horses for as long as they needed in exchange for their four and some help re-thatching her roof. He was immediately suspicious, trying to guess what the catch was, but she didn't seem to have one.

"We live quite far away; it may be some time before we are able to return them to you."

Her dimples flashed as she laughed at him. "Yer not very familiar with Aahvan 'orses, are youse? Just set the lot loose once yer done and they'll come straight 'ome." Aedrian grinned over at his brother who had joined them.

"What do you say, Aed? Nothing like a little manual labor to start the morning off right."

Aedrik was too busy being charmed by the woman's dimples and plains accent to respond. They flirted all the way back to her home near the outer ring of the town, Aedrian following at a slower pace and enjoying the innocent energy of this isolated settlement.

She showed them where the materials were, and they got to work. In Angerona, the roofs were made of the same strange stone as the rest of the city. Neither brother had ever thatched a roof in their life, so Aedrian decided to use his talent with growing things to aid their endeavors. Once they had everything in place, he made the materials wind around each other until the roof was sealed tight.

When they climbed down a little while later, she looked happy, but curious. "Well, I don't think anybody's ever dunna roof that way, but I reckon it'll hold longer than anybody else's in the whole bloody village! We don' get many tatties in these parts, but I sure am glad you two came!"

Aedrik laughed and chatted happily with her while Aedrian waited for the other two to join them. They ignored the racial slur, choosing to believe it was born of ignorance, rather than malice. Nevertheless, Aedrik's flirting grew somewhat more subdued.

Once they had everything they needed, they said goodbye to their new acquaintance. She insisted on giving Aedrik and Aedrian big hugs, joking with a wink that it would probably be a long time until she could hold men as handsome as they. She wished them well and stuffed extra supplies into their saddle bags despite their protests.

As they rode away, Aedrian found himself wearing a sappy grin. In fact, looking over at the other three, he found they all had the same expression on their faces. It seemed none of them could remember the last time they had been in the presence of a genuinely good and pure person. Those kinds of people didn't last long in Angerona or Tsifira. Their hearts considerably lighter, they spurred the horses into a gallop and practically flew northward.

The difference between these horses and their old ones was evident the minute they began to pick up speed. These animals moved faster than any horse Aedrian had ever ridden. He could feel their power in his bones and his communication with the animal beneath him was the clearest it had ever been.

"How are you able to move like this?" Aedrian thought to the horse beneath him who he'd learned was named Khaver. The horse did not truly speak but sent images in answer.

They were blessed by Magena Moon Goddess. Their kind had befriended the Aahvans many centuries ago and aided the people in exchange for the care and respect they deserved as gods-blessed beings.

Pulling up the sleeve on his right arm, he saw his glyphs pulsing in response to the power beneath him. That explained a lot. Of *course* they were magic. He should have guessed there was a reason these horses were coveted above all others.

Not many Aahvan Horses got as far west as Angerona though there was a rumor that the Angeronian Governor kept one in a separate stable from his other horses. Aedrian and his siblings had tried to find it when they were younger only to be dragged back home by a livid Deorick before they could confirm or deny.

By the time the sun began to set in the direction of their distant home, they had reached the banks of the River Leith, which ran from the Tamesis to the Eastern Sea. They started to slow their horses, preparing to wade across the shallow section ahead, but the animals had a different idea. This part of the river was narrow and shallow with relatively flat banks. The horses sped up further, alarming their riders.

When they approached the bank, their muscles bunched in preparation and—

—they launched themselves over the water. To Aedrian, it was like flying, but too soon they were touching down. He wanted to weep at the shear wonder of these creatures. As much as he loved the dark streets of his home, he was strangely glad their journey had taken them to this unexpected place.

They hadn't cleared the water completely, but they had avoided the deepest part, keeping the saddles and supplies completely dry. Aedrian turned at the sound of Aedrik's laughter.

"I guess they don't like getting wet."

Kilian looked a little shell-shocked, but the others were grinning broadly.

"Aedrian, remind me to go back to Aahva someday and give that woman a big fat kiss," Aedrian chuckled.

He wouldn't put it past his brother to do exactly that.

They dismounted and began to make camp. Aedrian felt the knot that remained constant in his stomach loosen slightly. A distance they had thought would take two days had taken just under one. They would be with Ashdan much sooner. Whatever was wrong, they would fix it, then they could all go home and finish what they'd started.

Chapter 38
Ashdan

Ashdan collapsed exhausted into the cell her mother's servant had thrown her into after the latest round of torture. While there were no marks on Ashdan's body, her soul felt shredded and tattered as she curled into a ball. She knew black magic took its toll on the soul, but hadn't been aware their mother had been *this* far gone. Looking into her eyes earlier, Ashdan hadn't seen any flash of affection or even recognition. No, Lorraen was gone, replaced by gods knew what. Everything made sense now, especially Deorick's betrayal.

She shifted her body painfully on the thin cot upon which she lay, trying to find a position that was even a little bit comfortable. She had no idea where Emyr was or if he was even still alive and the pang of sadness and guilt that came over her was almost worse than the pain of the last several hours.

Emyr was a good man and would be a great king one day. If her mother had murdered him, she would never forgive herself. Emyr was this country's only hope really, but it had been who knew how many days since they had arrived. For all she knew, he was gone forever.

As she had every night before she passed out, Ashdan tried reaching out with her mind in a desperate attempt to reach her brothers and Calloway. She hadn't heard from them for weeks as the distance between them had grown too large for actual communication, but she would never stop holding out hope that they had found Deorick and Kilian and were riding swiftly toward her. Ashdan hated that she needed rescuing, but her mother had put a damper on her magic.

She didn't have the Skeleton Key, so she couldn't even use a magically imbued artifact to escape. Her body, though whole, felt shattered and weak from what she'd been made to endure. There was no getting out of this without help.

Apparently, her mother wanted information on Aedrik. Ashdan couldn't figure out why she hadn't just *asked* him. Aedrik had always gone out of his way to please their mother. He didn't know what she had turned into yet and Ashdan was torn between hoping he would save her and hoping he would stay far away.

The one piece of good news—if it could be called that—was that Ashdan now knew exactly who the Daeva was and who was behind all of their recent problems. That it was their mother was some kind of cosmic joke that she couldn't yet find it within herself to find funny.

She prayed to the Faceless One, the nameless god of deceit, her patron as an assassin, to find her some way to come out of this alive. It was getting harder and harder each day to remember her purpose and hold out hope.

The next morning, she sat up, startled. Since they'd arrived, she had awoken every morning to the sound of the door to her cell scraping open with menacing intent. This morning it was the sound's absence that woke her.

Through a slim, barred window near the top of the back wall of her cell, she could look down the drop of a sheer cliff. The sun was high in the sky, but it's rays could not penetrate the shadows cast by the neighboring mountains.

At midday, food was pushed through a small gap in the door. It was shut again quickly with no words from the man on the other side.

Ashdan now existed in utter silence. There were not even noises from animals outside her window. The next two days were the same. Her voice grew hoarse from shouting—for her mother, for Emyr, for the twins, for anyone, if only to make some kind of noise.

On the third day—or was it the fifth? —Ashdan found proof that her feeling of the walls closing in was not just a feeling. Her cot now reached the other side of the cell, and her movements were limited to pacing small squares.

Ashdan shook when something changed for the first time in days. The air grew heavy and charged. She knew what that meant.

Mother.

Moments later, the door scraped open and Lorraen stood in the doorway.

"My dear, you look positively distraught."

"Mom? Please let me out. I promise—"

"Shhh, dear. There is nothing you can promise me that I desire."

Then what do *you want,* thought Ashdan. She'd never gotten along with her mother, but something was different this time. Lorraen looked at Ashdan as if she wasn't aware she was even a person—more like a creature that needed to be dissected and used.

Lorraen glided over in her finery and took Ashdan's face in her hands. A sense of calm and comfort swept around Ashdan, warming her deadened insides, and erasing her blind panic.

...This was her mother. She had made a mistake...

Her heart rate slowed.

...Her mother was here to help...

Her breathing evened out.

....She gazed into her eyes, seeing into their striking red depths like it was the first time...

Her thoughts slowed and ground to a halt.

...She had been so wrong. Her mother loved her and would never hurt her...

A contented smile spread across Ashdan's face.

...It was so obvious, she almost laughed...

"There, you see? All better." Ashdan stared into the beautiful red eyes of her darling mother. "Come, darling. Let's get you cleaned up."

Ashdan would do anything for Lorraen. After all, that's what family was for. She allowed her mother to lead her out of the dank room and up the stairs.

For a moment, she thought she heard someone calling her name—a man—but her mother stroked her hair lovingly and she forgot to turn around and look.

It didn't matter.

Only Lorraen mattered.

A second later, it was entirely gone from her mind.

They went back to the hall that led to Lorraen's chambers, but then turned down a smaller passageway. A flight of stairs later and her mother pulled out a key and unlocked a beautifully wrought wooden door. It opened into a plush bedroom, smaller than her mother's, but just as ornate and luxurious. Someone had taken the time to paint the stone walls a soothing taupe and cover them in tapestries and paintings depicting scenes in fields of wild flowers. Ashdan felt at home immediately.

Mother took such good care of her.

They spent a while chatting about nothing in particular. Ashdan told her mother how much she had missed her while Lorraen helped her in the hot bath. When she was done, Lorraen combed out her hair, leaving Ashdan nearly comatose with pleasure.

"Mother? Do you think the twins would like to join us? We could be a real family again."

"Of course dear, they are already on their way. Almost here. I expect them to arrive in the next couple of days."

She turned Ashdan around on the stool, so they were facing each other.

"Ashdan. There is something I need to know. You love me, right?"

"Of course, Mother! How can you ask that?"

"Because. I need to know that if anyone tries to tear us apart that you will destroy them."

Her face and voice were so serious and Ashdan felt herself drowning in those mesmerizing eyes again...

...Destroy their enemies...

She loved her mother so much.

...Of course. She would never betray family...

Her eyes pricked with tears at the thought.

...Anyone who tried to tear them apart...

Nothing was more important than family.

...Anyone who hurt Lorraen...

"I will, Mother. You may rely on that."

A beatific smile spread across Lorraen's face. Her pale hand cupped her daughter's cheek and she kissed Ashdan's forehead.

"Come dear. Drink this." She handed Ashdan a steaming mug of something. "It will heal some of the damage that horrible man inflicted upon you."

Ashdan shuddered.

"You saved me."

Sip.

"I did."

Sip.

"Good. Now get into bed, love. We have a big couple of days coming up."

"Yes, Mother."

Chapter 39

Emyr

Emyr had been stuck in this cold, dark room for days. No one had spoken to him and the only sounds to hit his ears were Ashdan's screams. He had initially expected that *he* would be the one tortured, but apparently Lorraen had other ideas.

After a couple of days, her screams of pain had stopped, but she had started calling out for people—her mother, brothers, him. He had responded, yelling back until he was hoarse and trying to comfort her in whatever way he could, but she didn't seem to hear him no matter how loud he yelled.

When he watched through the tiny window in his cell door as Lorraen led her away without any protest, he thought she might turn around and look at him, but Lorraen pulled her close, her glyphs shimmering red, and Ashdan walked on. The look she gave him over her shoulder made his blood run cold.

He was desperate. He had tried every conceivable method of escape, but he hadn't been able to find even a single loose stone. One time, he'd chipped a piece off with the corner of the mug used to give him water, but the stone had merely smoothed itself over.

In addition, his skin would not stop itching and he was being fed barely enough to stay alive. Finally, one day soon after Ashdan had been led away, his door opened all the way for a change and Lorraen stood in the doorframe. She looked as beautiful and terrible as the first time he'd seen her, but today she wore a pale pink dress that complimented her deep red glyphs.

He glared at her.

"What have you done to your daughter?"

"Nothing," she replied innocently, "she's resting contentedly upstairs."

"I doubt that. And the days of torture before that? How could you deceive your children this way?"

She didn't respond for a moment before she said simply, "Interesting."

"What is?"

"Two things. First, that you care what happens to Ashdan even though she kidnapped you and dragged you across the country against your will. Second, that *you* talk to *me* of deceiving others when you're lying to the entire country about who you are. I'm only lying to my children—as all mothers do."

"What? What are you talking about?" Her second accusation drove the weak defense he'd been prepared to give for her first point out of his mind. She gave a tinkling laugh. It should have been attractive—Lorraen was an objectively beautiful woman—but instead it sent shivers of dread down Emyr's spine.

"You don't know, do you? Oh, how delightful! I knew your father was a terrible king, but I didn't know he was so terrible a father." She giggled again. "Interesting."

Emyr was bewildered and his hackles were up as she insulted his father. What she said may have been true, but nobody said those kinds of things about his father without severe consequences.

"Here. Let me show you what I mean." She approached him and grabbed hold of his wrists before he could jerk away. They stood facing each other. She was the same height as Ashdan, he realized. Then he felt himself falling into her gaze.

Before he was too far gone, a pain up and down his arms jolted him back to the present. He tried to pull away from her grasp, but her hands were like iron bands. Her glyphs pulsed faster and faster. His skin bubbled and shifted. It felt like lightning was running up and down his arms. His eyes shut without his own volition.

Suddenly, everything stopped.

He opened his eyes and looked down at his arms, expecting to see raw and burnt skin.

His skin was not burnt.

Instead, intricate brown-gold glyphs covered every visible inch of his skin. He yanked the shirt over his head and examined his shoulders and chest. The glyphs were several shades darker than his skin, but they were not black like Ashdan's or crimson like Lorraen's.

Glyphs? What was going on?

Lorraen was wearing a satisfied smirk.

"You really didn't know."

"How? What? Both of my parents were human."

She laughed again and this time he thought there might actually be real humor in it.

"Were they?"

"Yes of course they were. My mother, Emylia, was the daughter of the Chieftain of one of the Northern tribes. It was what began my father's conquest of the North."

She raised a brow.

"I guess that is technically true. But that's what your father wanted the country to think. *He* is Unchosen, yes, but your mother was full Elymas. From my clan, in fact. Daughter of our Chieftain. We grew up together and I tended her as her lady in waiting when she married your father. I was the one who helped keep her glyphs hidden and I did the same for you when you were born.

Only I could have removed that spell even with the interference of the Nairna River. I assumed your father would have told you at some point what you were. But the spell also suppressed your magic, so maybe he thought it wasn't necessary. After your mother died, he blamed me for not being able to save her and banished me, so I was never able to tell you myself."

The tone of her voice spelled regret, but her eyes looked coldly amused. Emyr had never thought of the color red as a chilling color until he met Lorraen du Sonneillon.

Emyr stood there dumbfounded as she told her story. "You should be happy, dear. You will now have powers you never dreamt you could have."

That realization hadn't quite hit Emyr's brain yet. He was still getting past the surge of anger at his father's betrayal—How could he have not told him? And what was he going to do now? These glyphs were visible to everyone. Would the people accept a half-Elymas king?

Sparks shot up and down his arms—gold, instead of the blue, green, and red he'd witnessed previously. One of Lorraen's perfect brows rose in interest.

"Just like your mother. Everyone in the royal line has brown glyphs and gold magic. It's even more striking with your father's skin tone."

She reached out a hand as if she were going to touch him again, but Emyr jerked away. He found his voice again, but was surprised by the question that came out of his mouth.

"Your children's glyphs are black."

He waited, but she just stared at him.

"Why is that, if yours are red and their father was human?"

"Some types of magic can change you. I was born with black glyphs. Now they are red."

Some types of magic...she meant dark magic. Emyr processed this then asked the question that had been brewing in the back of his mind since she'd walked in.

"Why are you here? Why are you telling me all this?"

"Your father and I have recently rekindled our working relationship. I offer him protection and he stays out of my way as the Daeva. After he banished me and I worked my way up in the world in other ways, he saw fit to reunite us."

Emyr blanched at the way she said "reunite." He didn't even want to consider the infidelities his father might have committed with his mother's best friend, let alone Ashdan's mother.

She continued as if nothing were amiss.

"I have a feeling you and I can be even closer. You're a good man, but you're also a realist. You know that if the Rogue doesn't cooperate with the Crown, the Crown will not remain...alive for long. There would be anarchy in this godsforsaken country."

Even *closer?* Gross. It was one thing to lust after Ashdan, but Lorraen? No. Just. No to every word that had come out of her mouth.

"But you aren't the only Rogue," he argued. "Your *son* rules the other half of the country. Clearly, he doesn't know what dear old mum is up to or I wouldn't be in this mess."

"This is true. However, Aedrik is much too brash and unworthy of the title. I am going to take over for him—relieve him of his burden, so to speak."

"I'm assuming he doesn't know *that* part either."

Her smile was wicked. "Yes, well, disobedient children need to be taught lessons. Especially those who murder their fathers."

Emyr started for a second before remembering that her husband had been Rogue of the West before Aedrik. He supposed Aedrik would have *had* to kill his father in order to take over as Rogue.

He recalled reports from his childhood about Damian's Reign of Terror in the West. The man had been ruthless and unscrupulous. Rumor had it that the amount of people he'd killed made Ashdan's kill count look laughable.

Emyr's father had been about to send in the army to take him out when a report came that Damian's son had taken over. Somehow Emyr felt it was probably a good thing that Aedrik had done Damian in, patricide or not. Anyone who could be in love with Lorraen was probably not a good person. He wasn't going to voice these thoughts to Lorraen, however.

The throbbing behind his eye that had started as soon as he'd entered Sonneillon grew sharper. He winced. Lorraen's eyes flared, and he realized that she must be the cause. She was trying to delve into his mind.

Oh no you don't.

He had been trained to resist mental attacks. All royal children were. He threw up a mental wall as hard as he could, not taking his newly released powers into account.

Lorraen staggered back, as if he'd slapped her.

Instead of looking angry, however, she was suddenly grinning. It looked wrong, distorting her pretty face.

"Yes, I think we'll get along nicely, Your Highness."

If anyone else had said those words, it would have been a compliment. When Lorraen du Sonneillon said them, they sounded more like a death sentence.

Chapter 40
Aedrik

By the time the companions reached the Southern foothills of the Licean mountains, their light mood and amazement at the speed of the horses had long since been blown away by the Plains' harsh winds. Kilian had been keeping up a steady stream of complaints, ranging from "just let me out of the saddle for a bit" to "you're going to kill me anyway, why not do it now?"

Eventually, Aedrik had had enough and gagged him rather than listen to his whining. It wouldn't have been so bad, if the feeling the twins were getting hadn't suddenly changed.

One minute the feeling of pain and terror was getting stronger the closer they moved, the next it was gone.

Replaced by an utter blankness.

Since their sister had been born, the twins had been able to sense when she was feeling extreme emotions even from miles away. Now, it was like she'd been wiped away. That alarmed Aedrik more than the previous feeling. If they couldn't feel her anymore, was she dead? They urged the horses faster at the same time, leaving Calloway and Kilian to follow suit.

Pretty soon, they were wending their way through the dark valleys between the enormous mountains. The late day sun was completely blocked by the massive natural stone pillars around them, and they had been forced to light torches. Killian was now blindfolded in addition to being gagged.

Aedrik had always found it eerie to be in such pitch darkness only to look up at the light still in the sky. It was one of the reasons he refrained from visiting his mother as often as possible, though not the primary one. He stopped himself before he could go down *that* road. His guilt over their father's demise could haunt him at a more convenient time.

"Do you know where we're going. I don't fancy getting lost in here. Especially not with you three."

Kilian had managed to spit out the gag and was attempting to shoulder off the blindfold.

"Shut up." Growled Aedrik. Alerting the inhabitants of these mountains to their presence was never a good idea at the best of times, but they seemed even more treacherous than usual. Aedrik could only hope that Lorraen hadn't been delving into black magic too deeply. That stuff tainted everything it touched and lingered for centuries after its perpetrators were long dead.

Unfortunately, he had a feeling his hopes were in vain. Lorraen had stopped surprising him long ago when it came to her hobbies.

Kilian, who had been about to shoot back an angry retort, was silenced by a sudden noise high above them. The rest of them looked up, squinting past the glare of the dying sun and into the shadows. Either there was no longer anything there or whatever it was remained well hidden from their sight.

Aedrik would bet his life it was the latter. The air had taken on a distinct chill. He could see his breath in front of his face and Aedrian was pulling his cloak tighter against him.

The horses pawed at the ground in fright, sensing what remained unseen. He tightened his grip on the reins and continued down the winding paths.

Despite his distaste for their mother's home, he knew the way by heart and took pleasure in surprising Calloway every time he turned them down a path that had been unseen until they were right upon it. Aedrian silently brought up the rear. All three companions were holding their weapons of choice, leaving Kilian in the middle, tied up and blind-folded. The feeling of being watched had grown too strong for Aedrik's liking.

He pushed his horse faster.

As they drew nearer, the light bled from the sky; as if it, too, could not survive amidst such powerful dark energy. The movement they had dismissed earlier came again. This time when they looked up, they could see the silhouettes of human-like creatures prowling on the jagged ledges above their heads.

Glancing to his right, Aedrik tried not to acknowledge the sheer drop barely two feet away. They had left the valley floor behind ages ago. He couldn't even see the bottom—just endless swirling darkness. If they had to flee, there was nowhere to go.

Finally, they came upon the passage he'd been looking for. He made an abrupt left into the mountain, and they entered a damp cave littered with bones of small mammals. Climbing off his horse, he set the torch he held into a bracket on the wall. The others dismounted and ran their eyes over the dirt and damp.

"We're still half a day's ride away since the horses can't go full speed anymore. Even though there's no light here *any* time of day there are still creatures I don't relish meeting on those narrow paths. They only come out at certain hours, so we'll camp here tonight."

Aedrian nodded in agreement and began warding the entrance to the cave, the blue glow of his glyphs a comforting presence in the deep dismal place. Aedrik joined him while Cal took off Kilian's bindings, and the two began setting up camp and retrieving supplies for a cold dinner.

Their torchlight and the glowing blue glyphs combined to bathe the small area in an otherworldly green light. Calloway approached with two blankets, handing one to Aedrik and draping the other around Aedrian's shoulders. They both cast him grateful looks as they continued to place as many protections as they could on the entrance to their small shelter.

When they finished, Aedrian and Cal retreated to the back of the cave. Aedrik could hear their soft murmurs, checking in with one another. The gentle kiss they shared and the way they looked at each other made his heart swell for his brother. Aedrian deserved to be loved like that after so many years alone.

Later that night, when the others had fallen asleep, Aedrik lay awake wondering what they would find when they breached the formidable walls of Sonneillon. Had the Prince tried to escape and harmed Ashdan in some way?

No, that didn't seem likely.

Emyr was smart and resourceful, but Ashdan would never be fooled by him. Worse and worse scenarios began to fill his mind. Terrifying images of his sister's mangled body lying at the bottom of a steep ravine or of his mother thrown from her parapets flashed across his stubbornly closed eyelids.

When he awoke the next morning, Aedrik found his eyes crusted shut and a heavy exhaustion weighing down his limbs. It took several minutes before he could force himself out of his comfortable bedroll.

The others were already up and moving. It was hard to even tell that it was morning, but they had gauged a rough estimate from the time the sun had disappeared the day before. They walked the horses out of the cave before mounting them single file. Ears straining for the slightest sound, they continued on their journey, weapons and torches in hand. Kilian protested at being blindfolded and bound once more, but they ignored him.

Around what they figured was midday, they came upon another tall and thin crevice in the wall beside them. It stood beneath an overhang that threw it into deep shadow. Aedrik spotted hoof prints approaching from the opposite direction and continuing into the tunnel.

"They're here, all right. Those prints are several days old, but Mother doesn't get much traffic. They've got to be from Ashdan."

Aedrian nodded in agreement. "Whatever you do, don't lower your weapons. We don't know what we're walking into."

Kilian's voice interrupted, alarmed.

"Isn't this your mother we're going to see? What do you think's going to happen?" Aedrik shook his head and tried to ignore the creatures above who had finally appeared and now leaned in closer at the abrasive sound of Kilian's voice.

"Our mother is not..."

"Normal." Finished Aedrian. "She kind of lost her mind when our father died."

"You mean when you killed him," Kilian sneered.

"Yes, well, details." Aedrik spurred his horse forward into the tunnel, happily drowning out any further remarks from Kilian with the echoing sound of the horse's hooves on cold, damp stone. He was glad, too, to be out of sight of whatever those things were that had been stalking them from above. In the torchlight, they had looked twisted and unnatural. He didn't think they were created by the gods.

At least not by any gods *he* knew.

The others fell into step behind him, and he flexed his fingers around the hilt of his weapon, readying himself. Whatever they encountered in

Lorraen's home would not stand a chance against their whole family. He just hoped the four of them weren't too late.

Chapter 41
Aedrian

"Mother? Ashdan?"

"Mom?"

"Lorraen? Ash?" Their voices reverberated around the wide empty throne room. They had dismounted their horses and stood in the chamber, looking around for some sign of life. Kilian's binds and blindfold had been removed once more, but Aedrik had decided against re-arming him. The twins didn't visit very often, but every time they had, a servant or their mother would greet them as soon as they exited the entrance tunnel. It was as if the place had been abandoned, but Aedrian knew that wasn't the case. He still couldn't sense his sister, but somewhere, deep in the bowels of the fortress, he felt the slippery edges of his mother's mind.

Leaving their horses in what Lorraen used as a stable, they spotted the Prince's horse along with another they'd stolen from the Governor's Palace. It seemed ages ago that they had naively wandered into what had become such a grand conspiracy of betrayal. Aedrian sent his senses through the bedrock of the mountain to see what he could find. It was faster for him to use natural mediums instead of projecting his consciousness as far as it would go like Aedrik preferred.

This handy skill told him a few things: first, that Lorraen had redrawn the floor plans—again; second, that his mother was four floors down in what now seemed to be serving as the dungeon; and third, that she wasn't alone. She was, in fact, accompanied by two other warm bodies.

"Damnit!"

"I know. I can't sense them either."

Calloway looked nervous. "I have a bad feeling about this. I know she's your mother, but I don't like going in blind. I don't trust her."

"Neither do we."

"But what choice do we have?" Aedrian asked. "If Ashdan's in trouble, we have to help her." He thought he heard Kilian mutter something along the lines of, "or we could just get the Hell out of here," but chose to ignore the man. Vengeance would be reaped upon Kilian soon enough. Now was not the time.

"Let's go."

They trooped around the throne room again and again, Kilian's footfalls causing a racket, until they found the hidden stair. Aedrik muttered, "I hate how she moves them every time." Aedrian chuckled at that, recalling how Lorraen's penchant for playing tricks on them had driven Aedrik out of his mind when they were younger. She would often move stairs and doorways in their home so that they were forever trying to find the right one to take them to their destination. It seemed she hadn't lost her flare all these years later.

At the bottom of the fourth landing, Aedrian stopped and listened—with just his ears this time—and thought he could make out three distinct voices. He tugged the back of his brother's shirt before he could step out of the stairwell. Aedrik glanced back, a question in his eyes.

Be careful, Aedrian mouthed.

Aedrik shot him a sardonic grin and rolled his eyes as if to say, *that's not in my nature*. Aedrian cursed under his breath, but followed his twin. Gesturing to the other two to stay back, the brothers stepped up to the only cell with its door hanging wide open.

A steady light streamed from the doorway, illuminating the hallway and nearly blinding Aedrian as he stepped into the room to view its occupants. It took a moment for both of their eyes to adjust, what he saw when they did left him largely befuddled. He and Aedrik slowly lowered their weapons. Their mother was nowhere in sight. Indeed, there were only two other people in the room—Ashdan and Prince Emyr.

Ashdan looked comfortable, clean, and relatively happy if her blank expression was anything to go by. The Prince, well, he was a different story. He sat shirtless on a thin cot, but that wasn't the alarming part. The Prince's skin was covered in...

"Glyphs? Did they brand you—?"

Ashdan cut them off. "Boys! So glad you finally got here! We've been waiting for ages!"

"Ash, what's going on? We told you not to harm him."

"He hasn't been harmed. He knows the truth of who he is now. He's something more great and more powerful than he ever imagined he could be. Wouldn't you agree?"

Prince Emyr looked distinctly uncomfortable with this line of questioning. Or maybe it was something else, but he didn't seem to want to talk. Aedrian let the subject drop. There were more urgent matters at hand.

"Ash, where's Mom? We thought we heard her in here with you two."

"Oh, she stepped through one of the tunnels to go back to her chambers. She needed to change her clothes. She wanted to look her best for your arrival."

Aedrian stared at his sister. She didn't look like she'd suffered any great pain—there were no apparent injuries—but that sensation that had come to them over miles and miles of windswept plains had been real. Something had been causing her to feel agony beyond anything she had ever experienced.

"We're fine, guys! Really! Come upstairs. We were just going to bring Emyr up too, so he could take a bath." She wrinkled her nose slightly. Emyr frowned, but still refused to speak, making Aedrian even more suspicious. He held his tongue though, allowing Ashdan and the Prince to precede he and his brother from the room.

Chapter 42
Aedrian

An hour or so later, Aedrian found himself seated at a long low dinner table with Aedrik, Prince Emyr, Calloway, Kilian, and Lorraen. His mother looked resplendent in a midnight blue velvet with her dark hair cascading down her shoulders and back. The dress brought into stark relief her crimson glyphs and Aedrian noted that they hadn't been that red the last time he'd seen her. He also noted that she appeared to be the same age as they were.

Prince Emyr still had yet to say anything. He looked perturbed and Aedrian hoped to corner him sometime after dinner to get him to spill whatever it was he wasn't saying. Emyr wasn't the only one remaining silent, however. Kilian had surprisingly not said a word since he'd laid eyes on Lorraen.

Aedrian couldn't tell if he was in love or terrified, but it suited him just fine. He hated hearing the man speak. Needless to say, this dinner had been one of the more awkward meals he'd ever sat through. It mostly consisted of his mother attempting to make stilted and falsely pleasant conversation.

Aedrian wasn't convinced that everything was as fine as his mother wanted to pretend and when the dessert course came, his suspicions were confirmed. The bald, rat faced servant set small cups of a sweet dessert wine in front of each of them. Lorraen raised hers and everyone else followed suit.

"To this family. To having all my children under one roof again. To our accomplishments—past, present, and future." She finished speaking and everyone took a cautious sip. The wine was sweet and fruity on Aedrian's tongue. He typically didn't stray too close to dessert wines because of their sweetness, but his mother never served anything but the best at her table.

"Where's Ashdan gone, Mom?" She had disappeared shortly after escorting them upstairs to this room. Lorraen didn't respond. She was checking the clock in the corner as if waiting for something. Aedrian soon found out what that something was when Aedrik pushed back from the table abruptly and keeled over on to the floor, convulsing.

Aedrian cleared the table in a single bound, knocking over dishes full of pudding and glasses of wine. A candlestick or two might have gone down as well, but the only thing he noticed was his brother's face turning purple. He landed beside Aedrik and gripped his struggling head between his shaking hands, hoping to all the gods that he was not too late.

Instead of the usual finesse he might have used, Aedrian shoved his magic in its purest form into his brother. He forced more and more into Aedrik's veins, attempting to push the poison out. For it was most definitely poison. Aedrian refused to process the fact that his mother had poisoned her own son until Aedrik was out of danger.

He pressed harder, releasing more magic. Sweat poured down his forehead. He could feel his own body weakening with the effort, but just as he was beginning to despair of saving Aedrik, beads of noxious green liquid oozed out of the pores on his twin's face. Aedrian watched the liquid hit the carpet beneath them, discoloring the fine threads after several seconds. Aedrik breathed easier as Calloway wiped the poison off of his face. When he sat up, Aedrian noticed raw tracks across his brother's face and neck from where the poison had exited Aedrik's body. He wondered when or if his brother's face would ever return to normal.

Rage blinded him momentarily as he shot to his feet. But he had used too much magic saving Aedrik. If Calloway hadn't caught him, he would have fallen back to the carpet. He seethed as he stared at her serene face.

"Start explaining yourself immediately, Lorraen," he demanded in a lethal voice.

Emyr and Kilian both backed away as the woman stood. The servant stood in the corner; his face utterly expressionless. He hadn't even flinched when Aedrik had toppled out of his chair.

"Speak. Now. Mother." The sound barely escaped through his clenched teeth.

The smile that spread across her face chilled them all to the bone.

"You didn't really think I would let that brat run the entire west half of *my* country, did you? Especially not after he took my husband's life."

"*Your* country?"

She didn't respond, waiting for him to put two and two together. Aedrik spoke this time, his voice hoarse.

"It's you. Behind it all. I should have known. Nobody else could have convinced Deorick—" he cut off with a cough. "—or Kilian."

Aedrian shut his eyes briefly at the pain that shattered its way through his chest. His mother was the Daeva, the one behind all of their misery since Aedrik had taken over. It made sense in a weird, twisted way, but that didn't stop him from feeling utterly stupid.

He gripped the knife up his sleeve, thankful that at least their mother had never believed in disarming for dinner. He took a shaking step forward, but held his ground and shook off Calloway's hands. Pulling the knife from its sheath, another thought came to him.

"That wasn't Ashdan. Downstairs. That was you. Mother, where is Ashdan?"

His voice had risen as he spoke. Aedrik, Cal, and—surprisingly—Kilian had drawn their weapons on her. She turned to Kilian who looked as if all the blood had drained from his body.

"You failed me."

His face blanched and he started to back away, but she had other ideas in mind. A bolt of blood red energy shot from her hand and knocked him back against the wall, to land unconscious in a heap on the floor. The knife Aedrian had given him earlier skidded a few feet away with a clatter.

Lorraen's dark laughter rang out and her outline seemed to fade. Ashdan's form superimposed over her own as they both grew fainter.

"Find her if you can, boys. And tell you what—if you can find your way out of here alive, I'll *let* you go."

And she was gone. Gasping to his left made Aedrian turn. Emyr was holding his throat and coughing. For a second, Aedrian thought she might have poisoned him too, but then he spoke.

"Finally! She spelled me. I wanted to warn you, but I couldn't—I couldn't say anything. She did something to Ashdan. One second, they were torturing her for information on you, the next she was following Lorraen meekly up the stairs. I don't know what happened, but she couldn't hear me yelling her name. She didn't even turn around and I was ten feet away."

Aedrian put a hand on the Prince's shoulder.

"First things first. Wake that sorry son of a bitch up, take one of my knives if you don't have a weapon, then let's find my sister and get her back. If Mom wants to play games, we'd better play to win."

Chapter 43
Aedrik

Aedrik's face, throat, and lungs were still raw from the poison, but thanks to Aedrian, he was otherwise unharmed. He worried about his twin who had expended a lot more magic than he should have, but he couldn't exactly be mad as that same magic had saved his life from his murderous mother. They weren't out of danger yet, though. In fact, they weren't even out of the dining room yet.

They had moved to open the door and found it blocked by a solid stone wall. Not wanting to waste time or magic trying to blast through it, they had searched desperately behind bookcases, curio cabinets, and even pillows. Finally, just when Aedrik thought they might have to dig out the Skeleton Key, which had remained around his neck since they'd taken it back from Deorick, Calloway pulled aside one of the rugs and discovered a narrow trap door.

Noticing the servant still standing blankly in the corner, Aedrik grabbed him by the scruff of the neck and slit his throat. The bastard had given him a poisoned cup. The others looked at him with a combination of wry amusement and alarm, depending on their natures.

He shrugged and said, "One less enemy to worry about."

Calloway, Emyr, and Aedrian had thought to snatch candles from the dinner table to light their way. The longer they could refrain from using magic, even for light, the better. Kilian followed, rubbing his head while attempting to apologize.

"Save it," Aedrik growled, "we'll deal with you later."

They landed in a dark corridor and attempted to place where exactly they might be. Aedrik knew that if they took too long moving forward, Lorraen would change the layout again and they might be trapped for good. The Skeleton Key could only be used once every few days. If they were trapped too far under the surface, they would starve before they could get all the way to the exit.

So they moved forward, trying every door. Most were locked. Others opened onto walls as the one in the dining room had. They picked up the pace. Finally, as they were running out of corridor, Emyr opened a door to their left and called them back to him.

"There are stairs here! They go up!"

They hurried up the stairs, ending in a hallway with more doors. The only one that led anywhere was an archway that opened onto a spiral staircase. The stairs were going down this time.

They all looked at each other before Aedrik said, "Looks like we're going deeper before we reach the surface. Let's go guys. I'd like to get the hell out of here. Then I'd like to murder my mother."

He ignored the look of alarm that Emyr shot him. He would never understand.

They sprinted down the stairs and Aedrik noted that they went down not one, but two floors. They would now be one floor above the dungeons. Ashdan wasn't in the dungeons, was she? When they reached the bottom stair, they came out in another short hallway. This one had four doors—the one they came out of, stairs down to the dungeons, a fake door, and one other. The sight of two open pathways caused a momentary confusion until they finally decided to split up.

"It's not ideal, but just try all the doors in your new room and if none work, come back and take the other path. There are enough of us that we should be able to do that fast enough so as not to be locked out. Since the dungeons are the largest, I'll take Cal and the Prince with me. Aedrian, you take Kilian through that door. If anything happens, he has to protect you, or die."

The twins stared at each other for a moment before Aedrik cleared his throat and said, "Good luck."

He didn't know why he felt like this was goodbye, but he didn't voice the fear lest he speak it into existence. He turned and started down the steps to the dungeon. He heard Calloway whisper a few parting words to his brother then follow him down the stairs. Prince Emyr was fast on their heels.

As soon as they hit the bottom, Aedrik knew they were on the right track. The temperature had dropped, and the walls were like ice to touch. It wasn't cold just because they found themselves in the dungeon. Lorraen was warning them that she wasn't going to let them go so easily.

They spread out and began trying different doors. With only three of them now, it was taking longer, but it had to be done. They sprinted this way and that across the dark expanse. They even checked the cells with open and unlocked doors. Aedrik knew that was an exercise in futility, but given that they'd found the way out of the dining room under a rug, he wouldn't put anything past his mother.

Just when he thought he might have been wrong and had begun to tell the others to go back up the stairs, Calloway opened a door at the opposite end and was blasted backwards by the force of Lorraen's entrance into the room. She glared at them all coldly. The amusement that had been in her eyes earlier had disappeared to be replaced by a terrifying intensity. Her glyphs were pulsing madly. Vivid red sparks flashed up and down her bare arms as she stalked toward Aedrik.

"Did you really think I would let you out that easily?" She laughed harshly. "*I,* and only I, am the Rogue of Jesimae. *All* of Jesimae. I have seen your death, son. It comes at my hands."

Aedrik didn't respond. Lorraen had clearly lost her mind. There wasn't much he could do at this point except stay alive. To do that, he would unfortunately have to duel with another parent.

He drew his blades.

The ones that had been gifts from the woman standing in front of him. Two blood red blades materialized in his mother's hands as she continued to advance, mocking shadows of the ones he held. It was a long hallway and the trek to meet halfway seemed to take forever.

Neither of them had time for this. He and Lorraen broke into a sprint and charged at one another. Emyr got swiftly out of their way. In a great clash of swords, mother and son began to try and kill one another.

Chapter 44
Aedrian

Aedrian and Kilian entered the room off the hallway, filled with trepidation. They weren't sure exactly what to expect, but what they found was surely not it. It was as if they had stepped into a different world.

Taupe walls and earth tone drapes warmed the room almost as much as the fire crackling in the grate. They passed plush brown armchairs and shelves filled with books and at the far end of the room stood a magnificent four poster bed surrounded by shimmering, translucent gold curtains. There was someone lying under the covers.

Heart in his throat, Aedrian rushed over and pulled the curtains aside. Ashdan lay there so utterly motionless that for an instant he was afraid she had died. His fears subsided almost instantly, however, when her green eyes fluttered open and she smiled.

"Aedrian. I knew you would show up eventually."

"Ash, where've you been? What happened to you? What did Mom do? I can't sense you anymore."

She smiled benignly as she rolled out of bed. She was wearing her usual assortment of blades, he was relieved to see, but in a bed? Something was wrong.

"Ash?"

Her eyes snapped to him sharply. "Mother never did anything to harm me. Why would you think that?" He sighed. This was going to be harder than he thought. Had Lorraen wiped Ashdan's memory of the torture she'd inflicted?

"Well, she tortured you and tried to kill Aedrik—poisoned his cup at dinner. Now she's trapped us all in here to try and find our way out of her maniacal maze."

"Lies!" hissed his sister. She looked over at Kilian, as if seeing him for the first time. "Interesting." Kilian's brows drew together, but he didn't say anything. Apparently, he was going to leave dealing with brainwashed assassins to Aedrian.

"We should get going, Ash. We need to find Aedrik, Calloway, and Prince Emyr." That seemed to cheer her up. She appeared to forget his previous statements about their mother and led the way to the door. Aedrian paused and, just to make sure he'd covered their asses, checked under all the rugs and behind the armoire and bookshelves for anymore hidden trap doors. Nothing. They exited the room, Ashdan allowing them to exit first before swinging into the hallway behind them.

When they reached the place they had left earlier, they turned toward the archway they had watched their companions disappear through. It was still there, but the opening was blocked with stone. There was no way through.

"Damnit!" Aedrian yelled, kicking the stone and regretting it immediately. "We're too late!"

Kilian had walked to the opposite end.

"Maybe there's another way," he said.

The door that had been a false opening earlier now led to what looked like the armory. Kilian ran in without hesitation and grabbed something more substantial than the small knife he held, which he stowed in his boot. Aedrian nodded at him in approval. They were past their enmity at the moment. Everyone's focus was solely on escaping from Lorraen's labyrinthine fortress now. Ashdan moved into the room and picked up a stunningly decorated sword and belt.

"The Prince's weapons," she muttered. Something flashed in her eyes, but it was gone as soon as it came. As Aedrian watched her wander around the room, Kilian sidled up to him and muttered in a voice meant only for his ears.

"She's not right in the head. I'm pretty sure your mother's taken over her mind. It's how she initially roped me into helping her with her plan."

Aedrian nodded. "Unfortunately, there's nothing we can do for her as long as Lorraen is alive. She can hold her as long as she wants—destroy her mind, even."

"So we take Lorraen out."

Aedrian looked at Kilian in surprise and then grinned. "Congratulations, Kilian. You finally grew a spine." The other man blushed ashamedly, but continued, "only one problem. We still have to find Lorraen, and she could honestly be anywhere. She might even have left Sonneillon altogether."

"No. She wouldn't be able to pass up the opportunity to torture us. She's playing with us."

"Right. So, where would she be?"

"She'd probably go after Aedrik first. He's the one she really wants."

"So, in order to take out Lorraen we need to find your brother who is currently behind an impenetrable wall of granite. Too bad he's the one with that fancy little key—"

As they were speaking, Ashdan had crept up behind him. One sharp hit with the butt of her knife and Kilian crumpled to the floor like a sack of potatoes. She advanced on Aedrian, twirling her knife lovingly around her fingers.

"Naughty, naughty, Aed. Haven't you learned anything over the years? Plotting against Lorraen is never a good idea. She's your mother. How could you?"

Aedrian found it ironic that she looked and sounded genuinely betrayed.

"Gods, Ashdan! Come on, it's me! I don't want to fight you. Come on, wake up!"

But his sister was not there. She continued to advance on him until his back hit the door they had entered through.

"You will answer for your betrayal!"

Ashdan's famous claws shot out and she lunged at him. He ducked out of the way, and she spun around before she hit the door. She began to come at him determinedly. Kilian remained unconscious where he'd fallen. Aedrian couldn't hope for any help from him there. Under normal circumstances, he and his sister were nearly equal in skill. They traded off beating each other whenever they sparred for practice.

These were not normal circumstances. Any connection they'd had to one another had been wiped from Ashdan's mind by their mother's spell. She would kill him without hesitation. Her claws scraped across the stone with a nauseating sound as he ducked out of the way.

But he was slower than usual and narrowly missed being gutted by her other hand. The sharp blades sliced deep grooves in his leather armor and Aedrian began to think she might actually succeed as she came after him again and again. He was still weakened from overusing his magic to save Aedrik earlier.

She slashed, punched, and kicked, but Aedrian could and would not retaliate in kind. He would only dodge and block. Whatever their mother had done to her, she was still his baby sister and he would rather die than harm her. He threw up as many blocks as he could, but she was quicker and fueled by her unnatural rage.

He was thrown into a rack of spears and rolled out of the way just in time to narrowly miss being skewered by her hastily snatched up spear. She kicked him hard in the ribs, not giving him the chance to scramble to his feet. She kicked him again and again and again until he rolled over on his back. He looked up at her sadly, knowing he couldn't save her.

"Ash, I'm so sorry. I'm sorry we were too late to save you." He gasped in pain as her foot connected with his rib cage again.

Chapter 45

Emyr

Emyr had been in a few battles, but he had never seen anything like this. Lorraen du Sonneillon was the true embodiment of everything the humans were afraid of in the Elymas people.

Her beautiful form was long gone. She had become a shifting chaotic mass, taking forms of different people, animals, and monsters from his nightmares. At first, Emyr had tried to help Aedrik, but his magic was too untried and unwieldy. Aedrik had shot a bolt of magic at him, knocking him out of the way.

"Stay out of this, Highness." Aedrik gritted out.

That move had cost Aedrik.

Lorraen, who was currently in the form of a ferocious North Beast had grown massive fangs and stood on four powerful legs with claws tipped with a poison so potent, Emyr could hear it hiss as it hit the stone floor. She took a bite out of his leg with her powerful jaws. Aedrik's scream of agony ricocheted around the cold dungeon.

Emyr ran to the unconscious Calloway. Maybe if he could rouse him, Calloway could help somehow. He didn't have any magic, but he was one of the deadliest fighters Emyr had ever met. He shook his friend by the shoulders.

"Come on, mate. You've saved my life plenty of times. It's time for you to do the same for your friend over there. Please wake up and tell me what to do. I'm out of my depth here. Come on!" Calloway began to stir, but remained unconscious for the moment and Emyr turned back to the battle scene behind him.

Lorraen was back in her natural form and was locked in fierce hand to hand combat with her son. It figured that their mother was as skilled in combat as they were. Emyr supposed they had to learn it from somewhere. She'd manifested two wicked, blood-red blades that moved almost too fast for him to see.

And Aedrik was severely wounded and weakening.

Lorraen took advantage of this and kicked Aedrik in his injured leg. He fell to his knees only to roll back to his feet just in time to block a vicious swipe from Lorraen's right hand. The blades had melted away and she had sprouted actual claws. From what animal, Emyr couldn't tell, but he shuddered at the gouges they made in the granite when they missed Aedrik's head by inches.

"Why—" Shrieked Lorraen, "Can't you ever as what you're told!"

Each word was punctuated by another swipe.

Aedrik laughed.

"Aw, mom. I'm much too old for you to start disciplining me now."

In a split second, Lorraen's form morphed again. It was no bloodthirsty monster this time, but a man. Tall, broad-shouldered, older. His long dark hair hung in front of ice blue eyes. The face was scarred, weather-beaten, and cruel.

Aedrik's face, already pale from blood loss, went dead white.

"So that's what this is about?" He rasped. They stood, breathing heavily, eyes full of seething rage meeting those full sickness and regret. "You betrayed your own children because I killed that monster?"

Looking between the two faces, Emyr began to notice the similarities and remembered how Emyr had come to his throne. He had killed the previous one, Damian.

His father. Lorraen's husband.

Lorraen's voice came out of Damian's body, sending chills down Emyr's spine at the discordant sound.

"You and your siblings always were a nuisance, but when you took him from me..."

She shifted back to her own form again.

Aedrik responded, "He was evil, mom." He swallowed as he straightened from leaning on the wall and bento into a fighting stance. "And now I see that you both are."

Emyr had had enough.

He needed to get in there or Aedrik would die. At the beginning of all of this, Emyr wouldn't have cared what happened to the Rogue, but he had come to respect him in the short amount of time they had spent together in this hellish nightmare.

He told himself it had nothing to do with any feelings he may or may not have for the other man's sister. Seeing the alternative to Aedrik's rule as Rogue standing before him, Emyr needed to do everything he could to keep Lorraen from taking over.

He abandoned Calloway by the foot of the stairs and ran towards the fighting as it resumed once more with renewed ferocity. A sense of wonder swept through him as gold fire ran up and down his arms.

He didn't know what he was doing, but if he could just send a kind of blast at Lorraen to distract her, even that might be enough. He didn't get far. Before he could get more than twenty feet, he ran into something solid and invisible. The air in front of him flashed blue.

Aedrik was shielding him. That wasn't good. That meant he was spending part of his power trying to keep Emyr safe. He screamed in frustration and beat his fists against the barrier as Lorraen drew yet more of her son's blood.

His anger manifested itself in his new-found powers and he found himself accidentally blasting the barrier with balls of gold fire from his clenched fists. The fire came back at him, scorching his hands and pushing him backwards.

The barrier shuddered, but held.

"Aedrik! Let me help you! Don't do this!"

Aedrik's only response was a deep growl. Emyr wasn't sure if it was directed at himself or Lorraen who'd just contorted her shape once more and temporarily grown a massive scorpion's tail.

Instead, Aedrik's blade connected in a vicious swipe, severing the tail before the poisonous sting could reach him. She screamed; the sound unearthly in Emyr's ears. Aedrik followed quickly with a deep cut to her abdomen.

If that woman had once had any humanity, it was long gone. That was the only thing he could think of that would enable her to make that sort of sound. She retreated slightly and they circled each other, limping from their various injuries. Emyr was relieved to see that though Aedrik had sustained injuries, he had also inflicted many on Lorraen. She was a bloody mess, but then, so was Aedrik.

His eyes met Emyr's over Lorraen's shoulder. *Fine. Now you can help,* they said.

The barrier faded from beneath his hands, and he knew what he had to do. Mostly. He pushed all of his anger, fear, confusion, and uncertainty of the last several weeks into his power. It was like a warm golden glow that bathed him in energy. It filled him up until he was dripping with it, but still he waited for the signal.

A moment later, it came. Aedrik gave him an imperceptible nod and Emyr released everything he had at the woman who would see *all* of them dead if she had her way. Aedrik got out of the way as she was blasted forward onto her face. She tumbled through the air and landed in a heap.

Aedrik shot him a rabid grin and Emyr felt the same wild expression spread across his own face.

But before Emyr could relish in his accomplishment and first incredible use of magic, she was pulling herself to her feet. The crazy bitch just wouldn't give up and now her murderous glare was locked on him.

After expending so much of her magic in the fight with Aedrik, her true age had begun to show on her face and the youthful glow she'd had when they'd first spoken had disappeared. Her porcelain skin, now splattered with blood showed signs of middle age and there were streaks of grey in her raven hair.

He sent another bolt of magic her way, but he must have put too much into the first one, because she batted it aside like a pesky fly. The red fire that still remained within her pulsed up and down her arms as she stalked toward him and passed her son without sparing him a glance.

Aedrik had been leaning against the wall again, breathing heavily. His face looked ghostly and Emyr worried that he'd lost too much blood. As soon as his mother's back was to him, Aedrik pulled himself off the wall. If they were going to beat Lorraen, he needed to keep her attention away from Aedrik.

She sent a bolt of red lightning at him.

He threw up a pathetic excuse for a magical shield, not knowing what he was doing. But her magic must have been starting to fade as well because he was barely singed.

They continued trading magical blows until they were within arm's reach, at which point Emyr found he was about to have his fighting skills tested to the ultimate limit. He raised his sword and went in for the kill.

Or at least, he tried to.

Even in her injured state, Lorraen was ferocious. It was all he could do to block each blow as it came. There was an unnatural strength that jarred through his entire body with every strike. She backed him into a wall, and he lost sight of Aedrik over her shoulder. He blocked a particularly nasty swipe at his abdomen only to be hit hard in the face with the pommel of the knives she'd once again manifested.

He was knocked to the floor, and she followed him, kneeling beside his body.

Emyr gasped for air, knowing he needed to move *now* if he wanted to live. But the stars blurring his vision decided he needed to stay on the ground a few moments longer.

"You know; I can see now that you're nothing like your father, the King. This arrangement would never have worked. Such a waste," she tutted. It took Emyr a moment to remember the offer she'd made him in his cell just yesterday.

With that, she drew back her knife and prepared to slit his throat to the bone. Emyr wouldn't shut his eyes. He would die a warrior's death, staring into the eyes of his killer. A second later, he was really glad to have made that decision because Lorraen's arm froze, and her mouth gaped open in horror.

He watched in appalled fascination as Lorraen seemed to collapse in on herself. She turned her deadly glare back on her son who seemed to be pressing something to her back and grabbed hold of him with the claws that once more protruded from her hands.

Aedrik struggled to get free, but the talons were dug deep into his flesh. Their screams echoed off the stone walls. Aedrik used his last blade to stab deep into his mother's hand, forcing her to let go.

Both men stood frozen with wide eyes as Lorraen was sucked into some kind of portal. In moments, she was gone. Emyr felt the pull of the portal and scrambled away hastily. The movement caused an attack of nausea so severe, he shut his eyes in spite of himself.

When the portal finally closed, something clattered to the floor and Emyr, opening his eyes in alarm, was left gaping at the place where Lorraen had been standing just seconds ago. Aedrik stooped to retrieve the Skeleton Key.

The man seemed to have reached the end of his rope and didn't quite make it back to a standing position. He collapsed on the ground next to Emyr. Calloway, totally forgotten but who had woken up in time to watch the final moments of the battle, rushed to his side.

Aedrik was gasping as he handed Calloway the Key which had now turned blood red—the color of Lorraen's magic. Calloway tossed it to Emyr, seemingly unconcerned that the powerful magical artifact now also housed someone who would kill them all if she ever escaped.

"You—can't ever—use that—again." Aedrik's words were faint, but his eyes were hard on Emyr, who nodded in understanding. Calloway was frantically trying to staunch the flow of blood, but nothing seemed to be helping. Emyr slung the Key's thong around his neck and moved in to try and help.

"What can I do? Can I heal him?"

"Maybe, how much magic do you have left? I woke up in time to see Lorraen beat you to the ground."

Emyr glared at the other man who merely cut him a knife-like grin. "Not helping. What do I do?"

"I'm not sure. I don't have any magic so I can only go by what I've heard. When Aedrik healed me before, he kind of sank his magic into me and directed it to knit my wounds together."

"Right. Sink and direct. Got it."

"I'm going to try and find the others. Lorraen shouldn't be able to change the layout anymore due to her present state, so open doors will hopefully stay open."

He dashed off up the stairs he'd found just before he was knocked out. Emyr focused as hard as he could, placing his hands near the most grievous wounds. Aedrik's hand came up and grabbed his wrist.

"Don't. You'll overdo—it and—kill yourself."

"You'll die if I don't at least try."

"You can't—heal me. It's—too—late. Aedrian—can't—either. Maybe—you can put—me in a—magical stasis." Emyr remembered that Aedrian had used almost all his magic earlier to save Aedrik from Lorraen's poisonous dessert wine.

"How?" Emyr pressed. Aedrik was starting to lose consciousness.

"Same—concept. Sink. *Hold.*"

Emyr nodded and placed his hands over Aedrik's. He felt for his magic again. It was easier this time, now that he knew it was there. But there wasn't much left at the moment. He prayed to the gods it was enough.

He let every last ounce of his golden fire sink into the King of Thieves, letting it fill the dying man's body. Aedrik's eyes began to close, and he whispered to Emyr before losing consciousness,

"Save—them."

The light faded from his eyes and his hand fell slack to the floor. A final breath released from his chest before it stilled for good this time. Emyr frantically pulled his magic back.

Had he just killed the man?

But. No. There was a subtle shimmering coat of gold covering the other man's body. His power. It hadn't killed Aedrik. That final breath was merely paused. Frozen in time until Emyr released it or died.

He was at a loss. *Save them?* Had Aedrik meant his siblings? He felt utterly conflicted and surprisingly bereft considering he hadn't even known the man for twenty-four hours. He fell back against the wall next to Aedrik's body.

What now?

Chapter 46
Kilian

Kilian woke from unconsciousness—again—on the floor of the armory to the sound of weapons clattering to the floor. He pulled himself to his feet, snatching the sword he'd grabbed earlier. He'd been talking to Aedrian about taking down Lorraen and then, nothing.

A feminine scream of frustrated rage pulled him out of his reverie, and he looked over to what had previously been a rack of neatly stacked spears, pikes, and lances. Ashdan knocked Aedrian to the ground and began kicking him. Every blow she landed took the breath out of Kilian and he remembered the blood bond.

Shit. He had to stop this.

Aside from the fact that Aedrian was probably his only ticket out of this cursed place, if he didn't do something, Ashdan would kill them both with one blow. Ignoring the pain the best he could, he staggered around a table filled with helmets and different bits of very old looking armor, presumably scavenged from Lorraen's previous foes. He quickened his steps until he was directly behind Ashdan. There was a certain sense of justice as he brought the handle of his borrowed sword down on her skull.

She didn't go down immediately. She fell forward on top of her brother who thankfully had the presence of mind to grab her and roll until he had her pinned to the floor.

"Normally, I'd do this with magic so as not to hurt you—" he cut off as his snarling sister bucked and clawed beneath him, "—but I'm not feeling so magnanimous right now."

He hit her square in the jaw and her head snapped sideways. Kilian winced, feeling the pain in his knuckles. From how hard Aedrian had hit her, Kilian guessed that he had broken a few of his knuckles and possibly his sister's jaw. She would be out for quite a while, but just in case...

He searched the room until he found several sets of shackles, helping Aedrian fasten one set around her wrists and the other around her ankles. Kilian hoisted her limp body over his shoulder. His head was throbbing from being knocked out twice in as many hours, but Aedrian was in no shape to carry her. He was barely staying on his feet.

"Ok, so how do we get out of here?"

There were two doors at the opposite end of the armory from the door they had entered.

"One of them has got to go somewhere, right?"

Aedrian shrugged. His black look told Kilian he was losing the ability to care. That was dangerous. Kilian was supposed to be the useless one. As much trouble as he'd given the twins over their rule in the past, he was not a leader.

He had taken all of his orders from the Daeva—well, Lorraen actually—and look where that had gotten him. He took a deep breath and remembered what Aedrian had said to him before everything went to shit, "Congratulations, Kilian. You finally grew a spine!"

Well, if only to prove that statement true, he would take charge here and find a way out. He stuffed the sword into his belt and heaved Ashdan a little higher on his shoulder. Out of the corner of his eye, he spotted the Prince's bejeweled sword and other weaponry.

Maybe if he could find a way out, the Prince would reward him with it as a gift. After all, unlike the rest of their companions, he'd had nothing to do with the initial kidnapping. He held the image of himself owning such a splendid sword in the forefront of his mind as he grabbed it and headed toward the doors.

Before he could take another step however, Calloway burst through the door on the right. His eyes were wild, and he was covered in blood. Aedrian suddenly came to life and rushed over to him, cupping his face and scanning the blonde man's body for injuries.

"Are you okay? What happened?"

Calloway shook his head.

"It's not my blood."

It took a second before he could speak again and when he did, only one word escaped his lips.

"Aedrik."

Aedrian's hands move to grip his upper arms.

"Where is he?"

Calloway gestured down the stairs and they all hurried after Aedrian who had sprinted away the minute Calloway glanced in the door's direction. It was not the easiest to carry an unconscious body down a set of spiral stairs. It was all Kilian could do to prevent her head from smacking against the curved stone walls.

Privately, he thought she might deserve it, but knew Aedrian would gut him if any harm came to the woman. They descended lower and lower until they reached the dungeon level.

Before Kilian's foot had even hit the bottom step, Aedrian's anguished wail told him that whatever was around that corner was not going to be good. A crippling grief centered in Kilian's chest, and he realized that the blood bond didn't just cover physical harm. He stumbled down the last few steps and set Ashdan's body gently on the floor. He was surprised to find tears running down his cheeks and hastily wiped them away before joining the others surrounding Aedrik's body.

It looked like he'd been torn apart by a wild animal. He wouldn't really be surprised if that's exactly what had happened. Another wave of agony brought him to his knees next to Aedrian who was sobbing openly. Calloway's hands gripped Aedrian's shoulders tightly and his face was set in a grave line. Prince Emyr sat at Aedrik's feet and raised his head from his hands.

"He's not dead—yet. I put him in a sort of stasis. I think."

Kilian watched as Aedrian, a light of hope sparking in his eyes, shook off Calloway's hands and placed his own on his brother's chest.

"Aed, no. You are tapped out—"

Kilian found himself wanting to scream, "NO!" along with Aedrian, but forced himself to remember that though it was a grave situation, Aedrik was not *his* twin. This arresting grief and terror for a man he'd hated for the longest time was not his own and he could still function. They needed to get out of here. An urgent question occurred to him.

"Lorraen. What happened to her? I'm assuming she did this."

Aedrian ignored everyone. His glyphs flared blue as he attempted to heal his brother only to realize his magic really was nearly gone for now.

"I can't heal him yet." Aedrian's voice was a broken rasp. He gritted his teeth and continued, "But I can reinforce the magic Emyr used. I have that much left."

Calloway looked like he was going to object, but thought better of it. In typical fashion, the man's eyes shuttered, and his jaw clenched, but he didn't argue.

Kilian pressed again.

"Lorraen? Where is she?"

The Prince finally looked up.

"She's gone. We—trapped her. In this."

He held up a strange scarlet carving that looked similar to what Deorick had worn around his neck what seemed like forever ago.

"Is that—?"

He didn't need to finish his question because Emyr nodded. Aedrian spoke in a normal tone of voice for the first time.

"It seems Lorraen taints everything she touches. We won't be able to use that again."

Calloway nodded in agreement. Aedrian got to his feet and the rest of them followed.

When Kilian moved to pick up Ashdan again, Emyr stopped him. He stooped and lifted the assassin in his arms, cradling her as if she were the most precious thing he'd ever held. Kilian felt his brows raise at that, but didn't comment. Calloway lifted Aedrik's body, and they all turned toward the stairs leading upward once more.

Kilian brought up the rear, his muscles and joints beginning to protest now that the excitement of battle was waning. At least it was over.

Chapter 47

Emyr

On the way out of the Licean mountains, Ashdan had to be constantly monitored. Even though she had *moments* of clarity there were still times when she flew into a blind rage and tried to kill her brother. It turned out that Emyr was the one most capable of calming her down when it happened.

He hoped nobody wanted to examine that too closely.

A few days later, they reached the edge of the desert and set up camp. Kilian grumbled about saddle sores for what seemed like the fifteenth time, but went to set up tents without being asked.

Aedrian and Calloway gently laid Aedrik's body on a bed roll. As Aedrian and Emyr's magic began to rejuvenate, they'd taken turns starting to heal his wounds. He was thankfully out of danger from his physical wounds, but remained dead to the world. Neither of them was sure they'd be able to wake him up.

Ashdan stirred against him on the horse.

"Wh-what's going on? Where are we?" She said.

"We just left the Aahvan Pass. We'll camp here tonight and move on in the morning."

"Oh. Okay."

Her body stiffened against his and Emyr sighed as he felt the loss of her warmth against his chest. She cleared her throat, and he reluctantly moved his arm from its tight grip around her waist. Ever since Sonneillon, she'd been reluctant to dwell in his touch for too long.

A sharp ache flared in his chest. He felt like he was losing her. But that was absurd because he'd never had her in the first place. Emyr was man enough to admit he had feelings he shouldn't, but as she pulled away, he knew they'd never come to anything.

Ashdan walked over to where Calloway was starting a fire and Emyr tore his eyes from the curve of her hips in order to dismount Baela without falling on his face.

Her voice floated across the clearing to him.

"I can help cook tonight."

"No!" Aedrian and Calloway shouted at the same time. Aedrian continued, "Er Ash, no offense but I don't think we need your help."

"What are you talking about? I cook all the time at home."

"Uh yeah...and it usually ends with someone getting poisoned."

"But that's intentional!"

"All the same, I think we're good."

She walked off in a huff and sat by Aedrik's unconscious form and Emyr had to bite his tongue to keep from laughing. Somehow, this woman and her family had turned from kidnappers into tentative friends. He wondered what Aedrian had planned next.

Now that they'd gotten the information they'd initially kidnapped Emyr for, would they let him go?

The night continued uneventfully until they all settled down to sleep. Emyr, the one with the least severe head injury, ensured the others he could take first watch. To his satisfaction, there were no objections.

Things really had changed between them.

A couple hours into his watch, Emyr started to his feet when Ashdan shot straight up in her bedroll, eyes blazing with the manic fire he'd come to dread.

She made no sound, except to unsheathe the blades on her claw gauntlets. Emyr slid over to her immediately.

"Ash."

No response. No recognition.

"Ash," he said more firmly. Her eyes met his and he could see the two halves of her sanity fighting for dominance. His heart cracked a little, seeing her slipping away.

"Ash, you're safe. Aedrian and Aedrik are safe. There's nothing to worry about." He kept his voice low and controlled, hoping not to wake the others.

She let out a low moan and covered her eyes with the palms of her hands as she rocked into his chest. He placed his hands very gently on her head, more than conscious of the wickedly sharp blades at the tips of her fingers.

"It's alright. There's nothing wrong—"

Before he could finish his sentence, her head snapped up and she grabbed the front of his shirt. Her claws pierced the fabric and grazed his skin, but he didn't pull away even as blood welled in the shallow cuts.

She looked into his eyes and the panic poured off her in waves.

"What is it, Ash?" he whispered.

"Th-" she stopped, clearly struggling. The part of her that threatened the people she cared about was trying to stop her from speaking. But the *real* Ash was fighting back and forced the words out. It came out as a breathy gasp.

"They're coming."

Before Emyr could even ask, shouts filled the air and his vision was bombarded with the white and gold cloaks of the Elite Guard.

His father had found them.

Chapter 48

Emyr

Emyr had done his best to prevent any deaths, but the Guard had still managed to capture Ashdan, and Calloway as well when the faithful man had tried to help her. Aedrian and Kilian had fought their way out, not able to do much as they defended Aedrik's body. They flew as fast as they could on the Aahvan horses when they realized they couldn't save their friends.

Weeks later, Emyr paced his rooms at the Royal Palace in Tsifira. He had been trapped here since his return by a father who was desperate to hide him from the general public until his glyphs could be hidden once more.

The King had announced to his people that the Prince was home safe, but that he needed some time to recover from his ordeal. Emyr knew his father was terrified of him now that Emyr had discovered his true heritage. It didn't help that he couldn't yet control his magic well enough to stop the gold sparks from showing up every time he got the slightest bit angry. And since he'd returned, anger seemed to be the only emotion that came easily.

Barrett had been dismissed from his post as Guard by King Besian and it took a hasty intervention on Emyr's part to prevent him from being sentenced to death. It hadn't been Barrett's fault that the thieves kidnapped Emyr, not really. Emyr found he missed having the boisterous giant around and hoped to recall him to duty once his father had cooled down some. But this was pretty low on Emyr's list of priorities.

The others were still being hunted across the country, but Emyr didn't think anyone stood a chance of finding them.

Emyr had attempted to visit Ashdan and Calloway in the dungeons below Tsifira, but had been locked up as soon as he'd returned home. He was chafing at his bonds and wondering what was happening right now to the people he now considered friends. Just then, his father entered the room and Emyr glared up at him.

King Besian looked as though years had passed since Emyr had been kidnapped. His salt-and-pepper hair was now almost white and he seemed frail as if the weeks searching for his son had sapped some of his vitality. Or maybe it was that he had finally lost his son's trust and respect once and for all.

Emyr stormed up to his father and started to plead urgently, "Father, I beg you to show mercy. What they did was unthinkable, I agree, but it revealed to me my true self. They helped me and never harmed me. Please, Father. Surely that merits a sentence to the mines instead of the noose."

Besian was shaking his head before Emyr had even finished speaking.

"I'm afraid it's too late, son. The people demanded justice and their trial was held this morning. Their sentence was carried out an hour ago.

"You didn't even let me testify!"

But Emyr could tell his father had done so on purpose.

The grief hit him all at once.

Dead.

They were both dead.

The man who'd had his back and saved his life more times than Emyr could count. And the confusing, infuriating, murderous, beautiful woman who captured his every waking thought?

Gone.

A thought occurred to him then. What would *Aedrian* do now? Aedrik had begged Emyr to save his family before losing consciousness. How was he supposed to tell Aedrian that he had failed in carrying out his brother's only wish?

King Besian swept out of the room as his son processed his final words. Emyr was too distraught to even acknowledge his father's exit.

Epilogue
Ashdan

Ashdan sat curled in a corner of her cell, looking out at the surprisingly beautiful view of the water in the harbor. The shouting and jeers from their "execution" this morning still rang in her ears. Calloway had been tossed into the cell across from hers and he was really the only thing keeping her sane.

The longer she spent in here, the more she saw flashes of her mother's face. She knew she was losing herself—had already lost herself fully once. Ironically, it had been Aedrian's devastating blow to her face that had brought her back to her senses.

And Emyr. Emyr, who's soft voice and gentle eyes had pulled her mind from the depths of chaos. What must he think now? Did he know she was still alive?

She was fighting a battle within herself to maintain control, but it grew harder and harder to remember *why* she fought. Footsteps came down the hallway and she pulled out of her crouched position.

King Besian himself stood on the other side of the bars.

"Your Majesty, to what do I owe this honor? This morning was—interesting. Do you plan on doing any of it for real soon?"

The King smirked at her. "You won't be getting a trial, dear. According to all records, your trial was held this morning in front of a small crowd who will all testify that they watched you hang. You and your companion here were sentenced to death. Not only are you a wanted murderer, but you kidnapped my son and heir to the throne of Jesimae. You will die..."

The rage and confusion burdening her mind overwhelmed her before he could finish, and she blacked out. When she came to her senses, her face was pressed against the bars and blue fire was spilling from her fingertips. Besian raised an eyebrow as if laughing at her.

"That won't work here, dear, but it's nice to see you have much in common with your mother."

The mention of Lorraen had her vision going hazy again, but Calloway's head appeared at the bars behind the King.

"Stay with me, Ash. Stay here."

His familiar voice just barely grounded her, and she calmed down, taking a deep breath.

The King continued, looking annoyed.

"As I was saying. The question is not if you will die, but when. You see, you have a...unique set of abilities that I find particularly useful. If you agree to work for me, your sentence will be...postponed."

Ashdan spat at his feet. "I'll never work for you."

He didn't react.

"I thought you might say that. See, I'm familiar with *your kind* and their hatred of me."

He was referring to her Elymas blood, of course. They had been resisting the rule of Jesiman kings for a thousand years, demanding their rights as an indigenous people of this land, but Besian's hatred went deeper. It was as if his interactions with Lorraen had tainted his view of the Elymas people as a whole.

"I've decided to be generous here. If you agree to work for me, your companion over there will also get to live. If not, well, then he will die tomorrow at sundown and, shortly after, so will you."

"Ashdan, don't. It's not worth it."

Calloway's face was still pressed against the bars. He knew the same thing she did. If she agreed to work for the King, he would have her killing anyone who opposed him. She would be separated from those who kept her sane.

She would lose herself completely.

Ashdan remained conflicted, however. She could do this for Aedrian. If she postponed their sentence long enough, Aedrian might have a chance to save the man he loved.

"Think on it," said the King with a knowing smile. "You have until tomorrow at sundown."

She spoke up again. "Emyr—Prince Emyr—can I see him? I just need to—"

"I'm afraid that won't be possible. He has specifically stated that he wants nothing to do with you. Goodnight, dear. See you tomorrow."

The end for now...

Jesimae Book II
Memory & Mutiny

Coming December 2023!

Chapter 1

The Woman

To any normal person not brought up in the Royal Court, this would have been a once-in-a-lifetime experience, something to treasure and linger over for years to come. To the woman, the Midsummer Ball provided the perfect cover for her work. Whatever else her life had become—and she was having trouble remembering that these days—she knew her mission. Tonight, Ambassador Kane would die by her skillful hands as so many others had before him.

"Come, Lovely, it's time for us to move this party away from prying eyes."

He took her hand and pulled her into the cool, perfect night. No one paid attention to the Ambassador leaving with a beautiful woman and she found she was almost embarrassed by what people thought about to happen with this disgusting lumpish man. Sheer distaste and grim satisfaction warred within her as she followed him to his doom.

Tonight, she attended the Midsummer Ball on the Ambassador's arm—a pretty, yet unmemorable face amidst a crowd of indecent dresses and twinkling jewelry.

Heat shimmered in the air and the night sang with the whispers of a thousand nobles prying into one another's business. The atmosphere was decadent and sinful, just right for high summer—and for murder.

They ambled through the lush palace gardens, his hand creeping lower and lower on her hip. She resisted the urge to break the fingers caressing her over the fabric of her dress. Torture was not part of her routine—not tonight, anyway.

As they walked, the woman timed her steps with his so that only a single footstep could be heard on the gravel pathway at a time. When the lights from the party faded and the music and laughter left a pleasant hum on the night air, she deemed it the proper time to carry out her plan. The hedges of the garden maze hid them from view, enclosing them in a private world of their own. Only the stars would witness what happened next.

The man hummed as he swung her into his arms and she didn't have to fake her surprise at his pleasant tenor voice. She allowed herself to move to the melody. His eyes and hands followed the sway of her hips with unabashed hunger.

She leaned in, as a lover would, and rested her cheek against his. Sweat rubbed off onto her cheek and she barely stopped herself from recoiling. When she felt sure of Kane losing himself in the moment, she inched her left hand toward the pin holding back her tresses. She pulled it from her long, blonde hair and let it tumble in luxurious waves down her back. The Ambassador sighed with happiness and took handfuls of the golden threads in his meaty palms. He lifted his head to kiss her, but he never got the chance.

At that moment, she used the pin still in her hand and struck him in the throat. Nothing but a surprised gurgle escaped the Ambassador's lips as she lowered him to the ground. He stared with accusation and horror into her cold eyes, but the woman felt nothing. A sense of completion, perhaps, but no emotion troubled her as the light in his eyes dimmed. In the back of her mind, something fought to escape the confines of repressed memory, but she quickly stamped the feeling out.

A quick whisper and a flash of blue light and the blade was clean. She wound up her hair and re-pinned it. But as she skirted her way around the body to make a clean getaway, she heard a noise. It might have been background noise from the party, but the woman had not survived so long in her profession by taking that chance.

Let's Connect!

Find me online:

TikTok: @s.e.zellauthor

Instagram: @sezellauthor

Facebook: S.E. Zell

Website: sezell.com

Thank you!
Acknowledgements

A huge thank you has to be said to the entire crew from the Scotland writing retreat that gave me back my love and motivation to write. To my mentor, the indomitable Melissa Marr. To Haley (@hmmr.art) and Gabriela (@brosedesignz) for the amazing character art and covers. To the folks I zoom with every week who keep me writing. To my family for cheering me on.

And to you, dear reader.

I couldn't do any of this without your support.

Made in the USA
Columbia, SC
26 May 2025

58372021R00133